"You get yourself along home and get the soaps on in front of the fire. I've got to go in tonight because Mr Hughes is closing in the morning so all the staff can go to the funeral."

"Is there nothing you wouldn't stoop to, to get out for a pint? It's hardly Holy Thursday Paul, the pub might be closed in the morning but it'll be opened by mid-afternoon. Mick Hughes isn't going to do himself out of too many sales."

"Ah go easy sure I'll only be an hour behind you and I've no interest in watching Eastenders anyway."

With that Paul turned on his heel and left Maura standing there before she eventually turned away and headed for home. Tonight had been tough and tomorrow was going to be hard for her as well as Paul but all these years later he still felt like he had to shoulder the entire burden himself and protect her. But sure all the protection in the world couldn't stop her brain replaying the events of 1990.

****

"You'll have a pint of stout there Paul yeah?"

"Jaysus Charlene you could let a man in the door before up-selling your pints. But if you've already started pouring it I'd better drink it hadn't I?" Paul was well prepared for Charlene and her bartending skills. As he took off his jacket and hat he warmed his backside on the fire between entering The Local and getting to his seat, side on to the counter. That way he could see everyone entering the bar and be in position to be the master of all he surveyed.

"Are you buying me that pint as well Charlie or just pulling it for me?" Paul asked, knowing full well the response he'd get.

"What do you fucking think Paul?" Charlie lobbed back predictably.

"Funny I thought you might say that so I took my wallet out just in case.......and no, I didn't have to blow the cobwebs off first!"

"Are we a little bit defensive tonight Mr Forsyth?" Charlie asked.

"Na not at all, sure you know I only come in here for the banter because you can't pour a pint to save your life." One look from Charlie was enough for Paul to change the subject. She could give some withering looks Paul thought as he fished out a fiver. "I was down in the O'Neill's' there earlier and it's such a horrible state of affairs. It's not fair what's happened to that family. For her to slip and fall like that off the pier? It's just such damn bad luck."

"Ah it is alright Paul but how could the father have let it happen? I mean Brian's never going to win Mastermind I know but you'd think he'd have walked down the pier with her instead of letting her out the door on her own."

"Ah it only takes a second Charlie, he could've done everything right and accidents like this can still happen. I mean he was telling me earlier that he wouldn't have been holding her hand where she slipped anyway. There was just a bit of seaweed on the pier, she slipped on that and before he could react she was hitting the deck and rolling over into the sea. God love her, she was dead before she hit the water."

"But given all that, surely he wouldn't leave her out of his sight just in case something like this would happen?" Charlene asked

"Ah it would be great if it always went like that Charlie but accidents can happen even when you do everything right"

"Yeah but..."

"There's no buts about it Charlene and if you had kids of your own you'd know all about it. Accidents happen, kids get hurt and often there is nothing a parent can do. All you hope is that when they do fall, they don't hit their head or if they cut themselves, it's not too deep but truth is it's impossible to plan for all eventualities." With that Charlene was off down the far end of the counter. The pub was nearly empty when Paul had looked in the windows on the way in and he hadn't heard the bell on top of the far door. As Charlene wandered back up towards him, Paul asked "what did the invisible man want?" and with that he went in to a fit of laughing. Bloody hell he thinks he's hilarious Charlene thought.

"You'll have another one then Paul yeah?" she asked.

"Yeah one for the ditch, then I'm off. I'm under instruction to get myself away home within the hour."

"As if that ever meant anything to you Paul! Wouldn't take much for me or one of the lads to twist your arm and you'd be here for the long haul."

"I know you want me to stay Charlie but you've got to fight it, you can't stop me getting off home to my Maura."

****

5

As Paul pulled on his long coat and flat cap to be on his way to the funeral, he cast a loving glance to his wife at the sink. She had forgiven him immediately when he stumbled into bed after closing time last night. He really needed to give her some of his time. Today would be hard on her too he knew, too hard in fact, that was why she wasn't coming along. Paul went to everybody's funeral and generally Maura would go along with him but today was too tragic, too close to the bone.

Jack came bounding down the stairs and nearly brought Paul with him as he bounced into the kitchen. "Move it or lose it Dad, I've got to get the Weetabix into me if I'm going to get that job today."

"You need no more Weetabix my boy, 6'4" and 18 stone is big enough." Paul called out as he pulled the door behind him. How had he bred such a behemoth of a son? He being barely 6 foot in his prime and he'd lost height before Jack was born. 1990 had been a tough year, his posture had become woeful and he walked hunched over. He walked with his head down, never wanting to impose on anyone or anything. Even the arrival of Jack and Louise hadn't brought his strength and confidence back fully.

Even Jack's arrival in 1996 had been tinged with sadness. Without realising Paul had come to a stop at the front gate thinking back to that tragic day in June 1990. He pushed those thoughts aside and closed the gate. Children's funerals will tug on the heartstrings all by themselves; he didn't need to depress himself by bringing thoughts of Maura and their tragedy along for the ride.

2.

"I bet it was very tough today? " Maura asked. The words hadn't left her mouth before she saw his hunched shoulders. He shook off his flat cap and put it on its' hook in the hall. Instead of making him look younger by taking off the cap, when he took his coat off his rounded shoulders and hunched form made him look much older than his 59 years.

"Jesus it was terrible hard today Maura. There's no sadder sight than a packed church staring blankly at a small white coffin in front of the altar."

"You'll have a cuppa love yeah?" Maura suggested.

"Yeah that'd be lovely pet" Paul seemed to pause for a second before he ambled across the kitchen and, catching Maura off-guard, he hugged her close from behind.

"Ah for Christ's sake Paul, I'm trying to fill the kettle!" Maura instantly regretted not just her words but the tone that accompanied them. In 30 years of marriage she could count on one hand how often Paul had initiated any sort of intimacy between them. Other than when he came home from the pub merry and horny in equal measure. 'Why did I open my bloody mouth?' Maura thought as Paul sloped off in embarrassment towards the couch and the remote control.

"You're always banging on about me paying you attention but when I do you have a go at me and push me away! Can I ever bloody win?" Paul said these things mainly for himself as he was already halfway towards the living room and Maura was out of earshot.

Just before he walked into the sitting room, Paul paused for a moment to take a look at the communion and

confirmation photographs of Jack and Louise. Their
photos had been taken in the same church they had said
goodbye to Patricia in that morning and the cruel irony
wasn't lost on him. He had passed those photos for many
years and they had elicited many different emotions from
over the years. Today though, there was only room for
sadness. That was despite the smiling young faces of his
beautiful children looking back at him from the wall.
Louise and Jack had brought great positivity into his life
and they'd shared many brilliant experiences. Despite
those lovely memories they were all tinged with sadness,
guilt and pain for Paul. He gently stroked the framed
photos of his children, something he'd never done with
them in real life. As their parent he had been over-
protective to the point of paranoia and he'd never let
himself relax to enjoy those memories as they were
happening. Not wanting to torture himself any further,
Paul got moving again towards his spot on his armchair
in front of the television.

Maura was watching the heart breaking tableau as the
kettle boiled. She chided herself once again for rebuffing
Paul's intimacy. She knew all too well how difficult Paul
found it displaying any emotion. He hadn't always been
like that, in the beginning he had been loving,
affectionate and attentive. Somewhere along the way
though, he had become more stoic and withdrawn. She
had seen the changes happening to Paul but hadn't
known how to address it with him. Now she hadn't the
energy to confront him about it. So now as well as
missing the loving man she had met, she also felt partly
responsible for the man before her now. She came out of

her dreamland with a jolt and not knowing when the kettle had boiled, she flicked it on to boil once again.

****

Using her elbow to skilfully open the door Maura brought the tray into the front room. "For jaysus sake Maura, the Queen isn't coming over. What are you like with the jug and the plate of biscuits?"

"I only opened the 2 litre so I didn't want it all to get warm in here. Once I was using the jug, I thought the plate for the biscuits might be nice!"

"At least you didn't bring any sandwiches in with you. I'm sick to my back teeth eating sambos all week. There has to be a happy medium between soup and sandwiches and a full sit-down meal for after a funeral wouldn't you think?"

"Is that why you always put up such a fight for sausage and chips at funerals?"

Paul's sudden interest in changing the channel told Maura that she had hit upon something bad; she knew she had to plough on though.

"Look Paul, I'm sorry for the way I reacted earlier in the kitchen. You just caught me off-guard but I think we've got to talk about the funeral this morning."

"Maura, I've no interest in trawling through the details of Patricia O'Neill's' funeral. "

"That's fine Paul, I'm not that pushed about them either. I just know it's difficult for you to talk about your emotions and I know from you looking for a hug that it stirred up some emotions in you. I know I've been crying

9

this morning and I couldn't even bring myself to go to the funeral itself."

"Well I'm not going to cry if that's what you're angling for!" Paul exploded.

"Of course I don't want that Paul and I'm not hoping for it but if you felt like it while we are talking that's fine. I mean you've obviously got something weighing heavily on you that you want to offload."

"Obviously?" Paul snorted "Are you my psychiatrist or my wife now?"

"Ah don't be so bloody defensive Paul. You and I know you haven't given me a hug in years so either the funeral upset you or you're feeling guilty about an affair you're having? And in all seriousness Paul I know I put up with you but I can't imagine too many other women doing the same so I'm presuming it was the funeral of a young child which would naturally upset anyone."

"If I DO talk about for a bit will you leave me be then?" Knowing this wasn't the beginning of a negotiation, Maura knew it was the best she could ask for.

"I've been choking back tears all morning. I'm sure you haven't been because you never cry but the funeral of a five year old girl had to have upset you in some way didn't it?"

Paul turned the television down a bit. He wasn't turning it off but it was a minor victory for Maura and proof positive that Paul wanted to talk.

"Yes it was very hard this morning. I stayed at the back of the Church so I could make a quick exit if I wanted but I made it through the lot. The O'Neill's were crushed, Jaysus love them, and there's nothing anyone can say or do to ease their suffering. Neither Tara nor

Brian could do the eulogy so it fell to his brother Graham. It was so similar to Declan's in many ways. Nothing could possibly convey in any sort of eloquence the feeling in their family. Sure I went up to shake Brian's hand after the service but I don't think he even saw me."

"No probably not" Maura agreed "it'll only be when they look back at the books of condolence that they'll realise exactly who was there this morning."

"It was amazing too Maura how good it sounded when Fr. Murphy spoke about Patricia and the O'Neill family. He knows them all so well and it sounded so natural when he spoke about little Trish and all of them. If only that was always the case. I know there's nothing that can quell their grief but it must've been a small sliver of compassion and comfort to them."

"I'm sure it will be Paul, it won't be today or tomorrow but…….."

With that Jack came bursting back through the front door and into the sitting room. It'd been a long day but he still had as much energy as this morning when he nearly cleaned up his Dad in a whirlwind of nervous activity.

"Bloody hell son if you left the door on its hinges for another few years we'd all be very grateful!"

"Sorry Dad but you only heard the door yeah? So I got away with slamming the porch door then? Nice one"

Jack had a mischievous nature and loved winding up his parents at every opportunity. Not to say he wouldn't apply himself when he needed to, but he never missed the chance to take the piss.

"Go on, you can have that one so son but tell us how did the interview go?" Paul asked.

"It went grand yeah, not a bother……… what are you two doing in here with the sound off? Where you having a deep and meaningful?" he teased. "Will I leave you to it?"

Maura was about to agree but Paul was quicker on the trigger. "Not at all son, deep and meaningful? Us? You know the answer to that. Sit yourself down and tell us all about your interview. We were only talking about Patricia O'Neill's funeral this morning and how difficult it must be for the family. So we could probably do with a change of subject.

"Oh yeah, I forgot you were going to that this morning. How did it go? There must have been a huge crowd there for that yeah?" Jack asked

"Yeah there was alright, nearly the whole crew from The Local were there and most of the town was represented by somebody. The poor family were in bits but come here I don't really want to be talking about that. For about the third bloody time, how did the interview go?"

"Deadly so it was, well sorry that's probably not a very appropriate word but yeah I was really happy with how it went. I'd be fairly confident I'll at least be getting a call back."

"Well done son, I'm proud of you" Paul enthused.

"Absolutely James that's great news" Maura agreed.

"James mam? Really? I'm saying the interview went well and you don't know my name?!" Jack was loving the opportunity to wind his mother up. "I know you're getting older and the Alzheimer's is kicking in but that's an easy one to remember. There's only me and Louise so I suppose I'll only start getting worried about you if you start calling me Lou."

"Yeah sorry son, just a slip of the tongue. I am very proud of you for going out and getting an interview when there's not many about and then giving it your best shot." Maura mumbled but she was embarrassed at her slip.

"Yeah I'll echo that my boy" Paul said, hoping to move on, "I never thought you had it in you to get up off your fat arse and look for a job."

"Fat arse? You can call me lots of things Da but this arse is as finely sculpted as they come"

"Fair enough I'll change that. You're just a lazy arse then. Does that make you feel better?"

"Listen I don't need to stay here being called the wrong name and getting slagged off." Jack teased. "I'm going for a shower and then down The Local for a pint. They'll be open by now Dad won't they? I know they were at the funeral but Mr. Hughes won't miss out on any more takings will he?"

"Definitely not, Jackie boy, I think I heard him say they'd be re-opening at 5."

"Nice one" Jack said and just as he put his hand on the door and before he ran up the stairs he decided to chance his arm. "Any chance of a few quid for my pints Da? I mean I'll pay you back when I get the job but I'm having a bit of a cash flow issue at the moment!" with that he was gone, running up the stairs.

"Oh God Paul, I'm really losing it. Where did that slip up come from? I'm just glad I've always got these rosy cheeks or you would have seen just how embarrassed I was."

"Relax would you Maura? It could happen to anyone and all it does is give him some more ammunition to throw at you when he thinks you're going senile."

3.

Charlie stood behind the cards of peanuts and crisps, listening to Paul and Padraig's row developing. She knew Paul was in no mood for talking this morning. Twenty years serving his pints on a Sunday morning had taught her that. Four pints, half an hour over each one, about 20 words and a blessing of his pint was as good as it got on a Sunday morning.

The rest of the week Paul could be a jovial enough character but Sundays didn't suit him. Maybe it was the extra customers upsetting his routine but rarely had he relaxed and enjoyed the banter as he could during the rest of the week. She often wondered was it a religious thing but he never really came across as the God-fearing type and he started every sentence with jaysus this or jaysus that.

"For jaysus sake son, take the cloth out of your ears. Maybe Charlene is trying to protect the confidence of a customer by not telling you the whole truth!" Paul shouted at Padraig.

"For fucks sake! This town and its bloody secrets! I've been drinking here for a while and I'm still the outsider, the bloody newbie."

"And it'll continue for longer too. This town is no suburb of Dublin and we're comfortably insular. We've never liked outsiders coming up here poking their noses in our business. Just ask the bleedin' black and tans about that."

"Yeah I'd noticed but I'm not like that" Padraig continued. "I thought it'd be different for me being Irish and all. I'm not some African asylum seeker or a newcomer from Eastern Europe. I'm from fucking

Fermanagh not Nairobi or Poznan and I'm still not welcomed. All I wanted to know was why I couldn't get a bloody pint on Wednesday morning?"

"Do you really want to know? Do you? Right then I'll tell you. Brian O'Neill, you know the kind-hearted, softly spoken gent of a man who sits there by the front door?" Padraig tried to answer but Paul wasn't for stopping. "Well his little pride and joy Patricia died last Saturday and we buried the poor child, Jaysus be good to her, on Wednesday morning. If you were a local, or even trying to be, you would have sensed the air in the town, you'd have seen the tears in peoples' eyes, fuck it you'd have overheard the conversations in here. But no, you're so far up your own backside and caught up in your own life you couldn't or just didn't notice!"

Truth was Padraig was careful not to notice these things or ask the locals what had happened. If he opened himself up like that, that door could never be closed again and he wouldn't let that happen. Not again.

"Bloody hell, I didn't know any of that and had I, I definitely wouldn't have….."

"No you didn't know you insensitive prick!" Paul interrupted "so just be careful in future what you say."

"Hey that's out of line, I didn't know. That can happen to anyone and it's not as if it was your daughters' funeral or that bitch of a barmaid's daughter that died."

Paul's stool was on the ground making an awful noise before he was aware of it. 'What the hell are you going to do when you get to him?' he thought 'You've never thrown a punch in your life.' Padraig stood up by reflex and approached Paul. He'd only ever thrown one punch and that hadn't gone well at all. As they got closer Padraig hoped it wouldn't come to that.

Charlie broke into a run, her hangover gone in an instant. There wasn't really much she'd be able to do but she had to get out there in between them and hope that neither would want her to get an accidental blow. It was just as well they'd been sitting at opposite ends of the counter and were taking so long to get to each other. 'Maybe their hearts aren't really in it either' she thought. These lads don't want to fight and certainly don't know how to. She felt they both wanted her to intervene and they were giving her plenty of time to do so. She'd seen enough bar fights and brawls in pubs to know that if anything was going to happen, it happened instantly and unless a wrestling match developed, it was generally over before the bar staff got there.

This would never be a fight but for it all to look real and the lads to keep their dignity, she wouldn't be able to stop it herself. There were a few other customers about this morning but with their combined ages well above four figures nobody was about to jump in and help.

The front door of The Local is in the centre of the bar counter. For years and years the customers were divided into those that drank at the top and those who drank at the bottom. No local had ever sat on the centre stool that straddles North and South. So when Derek Flynn burst through the front door he found himself right between the two men. Knowing Paul and how he couldn't hurt a fly, Derek presumed the other man to be at fault and grabbed him. He knew Charlie would be able to talk Paul down and chill him out.

"I was having a smoke outside there Charlie when I saw these two featherweights sizing each other up." Derek explained. "Aren't you glad your hero was here to save you?"

Normally Charlie would be loath to agree but on this occasion his arrival had proved useful. "You're a real knight in shining armour so you are, but get out of my bar with that smoke in your hand and bring your man with you."

"Why am I being thrown out? He's as much at fault as I am, he came for me!" Padraig was feeling particularly aggrieved.

"I'm not fucking barring you your highness, just go home for today and I'll get your version next time you're in. Get him out of here Derek."

Padraig tried to protest but at about 17 stone Derek could have snapped him like a twig so with discretion being the better part of valour, he sloped off towards home. The good thing about Kilcastle is he only had to head towards home and not actually to home. One of the towns 6 other pubs would get a few quid off him before then.

****

Derek stood outside The Local finishing his cigarette. As he did he watched the angry customer barge through McCourt's door. They would put up with less messing up there but Derek didn't think he'd be causing anymore hassle today. As he turned to enter the pub, Paul and Charlie happened to look up at him at the same time. He flashed them a toothy, smoke stained grin and polished his imaginary halo. They simultaneously shook their heads and went back to their conversation. 'Fuck that' thought Derek 'I'm the hero of the hour here and I'm going to milk this for everything I can.'

"Here he comes to save the day!" Derek bellowed. Just in case any of the old codgers had been asleep and missed his heroics he wanted to make sure they all had the chance to acknowledge his bravery.

"Shut up Derek! Your timing was good but you hardly took a bullet protecting the President." Charlie countered.

"Bloody hell, it's a tough crowd in here. And what about you Rocky? Sorry Paul, are you not going to thank me for saving you?"

"You hardly saved me," Paul replied.

"Maybe not but you were giving him what? 50 years? Weren't you?" Derek looked around the pub for the hearty chuckles which never came from his invisible audience.

"See this pint?" Charlie asked by way of interrupting Derek. "See this pint? Right? There are two more just like it in the taps for "saving" me and Paul if you take it, bugger off down the bottom of the pub and leave me and Paul to talk about what happened; you got it?"

Derek considered negotiating a better deal but afraid he might lose out on the other two he decided to take his pint of Stella and leave them to it. As he passed the front door Sean Robinson was the unfortunate one to walk in next. "Robbo," Derek began "wait 'til you hear how I stood between Rocky and Ali this morning to protect my Charlie." Derek's arm on his shoulder gave Sean little choice but to follow him and not ignore the welcome.

"Right Paul, what was all that about this morning? I've never known you to lose your head like that."

"Ah I know Charlie and I'm sorry love. He just wound me up something shocking but it's just as well that free-loader Derek turned up when he did. I don't know how to fight and I definitely wouldn't want anything like that to happen in here."

"Go easy on the free-loader stuff Paul. That muppet will be telling everyone of his bravery for weeks but I was glad he came in when he did."

"Ah jaysus you're not serious Charlie? I thought you had more sense than that. He's nothing but trouble, a fucking bad smell."

"He just has a certain hold on me from way back and he could be a bit of a charmer. But enough of my life why were you gunning for your man?"

"Believe it or not I was protecting your name Charlie."

"Me?"

"Yeah as soon as you headed for the cold room he started on about you. 'That hung-over bitch won't give me a straight answer. All I wanted was a pint on the way home from work.' Now I knew you were hung-over alright. You forget I can feel the draught when you go into the bottle store with the glass of ice to your head don't you?" Paul was back to the teasing and the winding-up that she knew but she was a little disappointed he knew her hangover routine.

"You know I don't mind anyone being hung-over, you're just as entitled as anyone else to have a few drinks but you're no bitch. A moody cow maybe but I know you only put on the bitch routine when you need to."

"Ah would you fuck off Paul, I don't put anything on. You have to be tough working in a pub and twice as thick skinned when you're a woman behind the counter. I need that thick skin and a sharp tongue to survive!"

"I know, I know, I was only teasing but you can't resist diving in can you?" Paul was chuckling again. "But seriously I know you were protecting Brian's privacy. God bless his soul, he was a wreck and so were the whole family on Wednesday but he's gonna have to be tough for the whole family now. If your man didn't know about it, I didn't want to blab and have him awkwardly approach Brian next time he's in for a quiet pint, reminding him of his troubles. But he just kept at it and I snapped at him just to shut him up."

"Don't worry Paul, I know you were trying to do your best by Brian and he wouldn't have let it go 'til you told him."

"Yeah you're probably right but Brian doesn't need people he doesn't know or care about commiserating with him for weeks to come. I mean it'll be hard enough for him to carry on as it is…." Paul tailed off and for the second time Charlie noticed the corners of his eyes fill with small but unmistakeable tears.

As she had brought him back towards his upturned stool and handed him his fallen wallet, she had noticed moistness in his eyes she'd never seen before. This man who loved a wind-up but was also so stoic had let his guard down twice in no time at all. As Charlie brought Derek his second pint of Stella she wondered what that was all about.

4.

Derek Flynn sat, as he always did, in the bottom of The Local. He was born without a problem to his name but had cultivated and fed the chip he carried on his shoulders these days. Contrary, awkward and, though a local, always viewed as an outsider, as being a little odd and a stranger in his own town.

It all started when Derek was 16 and nobody was in any doubt that his anger and frustration with the world began to grow at the same time his academic struggles kicked in. In a small town with no hiding places, except in the bottom of a glass, someone will be known as the brightest, another, the most athletic and yet another, the most musical. Unfortunately there is always someone who will be most likely to struggle after leaving school. Being average, at best, in almost everything he did even Derek recognised that this was to be his role in life. In some ways he relished being known for something. Did he wish to be known for something more positive? Of course but once he realised attention and fame came with the notoriety, he played up to his casting as disruptive class clown with great commitment. With more application than he'd shown to anything else.

In the course of a single year, Derek went from being comfortably in the middle of the pack to failing exams regularly and dropping like a stone through the ratings. What frustrated his teachers most was not so much that he was failing but that if he had applied himself, even a little, he could have stayed innocuously amongst the average. But again and again he refused to do so and played up for the attention. Better to be known for something, even negatively, than to be anonymously in the also-rans; or so Derek believed anyway.

The only exception to this came at Christmas in 1998. For three whole weeks leading up to Christmas Derek applied himself with improved dedication. He began to put his hand up with answers to questions rather than the one-liner replies that brought a cheap laugh from his classmates. He became the hard working student once again and his teachers hoped he had turned a corner. They hoped for it but they had too much experience of teenagers and knew it probably wouldn't last. As quickly as the positive change came on his behaviour deteriorated again, this time for good. In the space of the school holiday he returned to being the withdrawn, disinterested young man again. They all felt it was a terrible waste of his abilities but none could find a way to get inside his head to encourage and motivate him to apply himself rigorously.

Derek was like so many others in provincial Ireland of the late 1990's. He knew he had some ability but it wasn't enough to take him out of his town for better things. There wasn't enough to get him to college or help him into a good job to help him spread his wings and mature. Consequently he walked out of St. Malachys in May 1999 just weeks before his Leaving Certificate.

As he held his pint of Stella, Derek thought back on those days. How he had decided if he wasn't going to use his Leaving Cert then why should he bother putting himself under that pressure? 'It wasn't a bad time for you though was it kid? Beating the other kids to the jobs market by a few weeks' he thought to himself while supping his pint. He had found a summer job with a gardener in the town but he was far from a gardener. Instead he spent the beautiful summer astride a ride-on mower keeping the new estates perfectly manicured. The world famous Celtic Tiger got them property management and local authority contracts, plenty to keep them busy.

When the autumn rolled around Derek's old classmates headed off to college or training, getting to Dublin and opening up the world for themselves. Meanwhile he kept cutting grass, raking in a relative fortune. 'How many times did we use that shit pun? But they were great days, money coming in, no bills or commitments and all the nights out you wanted!' This last thought reminded Derek he was nearly through his pint of Stella.

"Charlie my dear, a pint of your finest Stella when you're ready"

"Yeah when I'm ready you'll get it, alright?" Charlie was busy restocking the shelves and fridges after the weekends' trade. 'The joys of Monday afternoons' she thought 'cleaning up after the weekend and serving all one of my customers.'

"What has you in here on a Monday afternoon pissing me off?" Charlene asked while pouring his pint.

"Great result in Dundalk yesterday evening, €100 it was worth to me!"

"So you've decided to hand it over as a charitable donation to poor Mr. Hughes?"

"Ah just some of it…. and of course to keep you entertained while you toil away!"

"Such a gentleman you are! One pint of wife beater" she said, placing his pint on the counter. "You know you were laughing out loud earlier. You're a fuckin' weirdo anyway but laughing on your own?"

"Didn't realise I was but yeah I was just thinking back on school and my summer with Gerry the gardener."

"Hilarious I'm sure!" Charlie snorted as she picked up his money.

"I was also thinking about you and me and that great month we had together over Christmas 1998. That was a fun month wasn't it babes? I tell you what, you thought me some great tricks back then." Derek was smiling again, a dirty, lewd grin full of innuendo and sleaze. But Charlie wasn't.

"Don't you fucking dare talk about that terrible mistake I made!" said Charlie while slamming the till drawer.

"You were a screw up then and you're the same now. Do you think I want anyone knowing we went out? Even if it was only for a month when we were kids. Are you hearing me or do you need me to write you a fuckin' note?" She was up in Derek's face now, shouting at him and an angry vein pulsing at her temple.

"You're so beautiful when you're angry Charlie!" Derek teased.

"I'm not messing Derek, don't you dare bring that up again. I thought when you pissed off to Scotland I'd be able to get past it but now you've gone and come home. I'm going out to get a case of beer and when I'm gone, you're going to drop that subject and you'll never bring it up again, right?"

Charlie turned on her heel and headed for the storeroom. Derek had always loved the fire and anger she had but he knew this wasn't something to test her with. He'd drop the subject for now but it'd be a handy joker in the pack another time.

Suitably chastised Derek felt his composure return as he saw Padraig's head pass the window. Time for a bit of fun he thought and he began as soon as Padraig put his hand on the door.

"There he is now, the flyweight champion of the world! He floats like a butterfly and stings like when you pee! Introducing the non-punching, most polite fighter it is Rocky, Iron-Mike, Mohammed Ali, Collins!!!"

Padraig was mortified. The last thing he wanted to do was get into scrapes and he wanted to put yesterday's messing firmly in the past. "Don't be starting with that now, I'm here to apologise so don't you be stirring the pot."

"Bloody hell what's with everyone declaring topics off limits this morning? Someone's going to have to send me an email with a list of safe discussion subjects in the pub." Derek went back to his pint, shaking his head at the lack of audience for him to command.

"Is Charlene here?" Padraig continued determined to get through what he had come to say.

"Yeah she is mate but she's hiding from me for a while so you may as well park it for a while. We never got around to introductions yesterday. I'm Derek" he said, gesturing to the sit beside him and extending his hand towards Padraig.

With few enough friends in the town yet, Padraig couldn't afford to rebuke his offer. Shaking hands, Padraig slipped on to the stool beside Derek in the bottom of The Local.

"So what happened yesterday Rocky? Was Paul threatening to run off with Adrienne?" Derek was laughing again, 'Jesus I don't know how I think of them' he thought to himself.

"Listen, enough with the nicknames Derek. I'm no fighter and I certainly don't want to shit on my own doorstep and have any trouble in the pub I want to drink in. Charlene will accept my apologies won't she?"

"Of course she will, ye mad yoke! All you did was have words with an old fool. I'm sure he's as ashamed of it as you seem to be." Derek replied.

This made Padraig feel a little better but he still wanted to get through his apology and get it out of the way. He stood up as if to take a look in to the back stores from the middle of the counter but Derek just sat there laughing at him again. It was really beginning to wind Padraig up but he had him worked out quickly. 'He must be the pub jester' Padraig thought 'more laughed AT than WITH'. As Derek pulled him by the coat and told him to sit down again, Padraig wished Charlie would hurry back. He would have no such luck.

"Come here 'til I give you some advice young buck. I'll give you the background on this pub and its' cast of characters. I know them all; the talkers, the drinkers, the fighters, the old ones and the new. If you want to know anything about this pub just ask the oracle here."

"Oracle me hole!" was how Charlie announced her return to the counter. She emerged from the back stores with a case of Budweiser. "Didn't you fuck off to Scotland for 5 years? What would you know about all the locals of this town? And while I'm at it" she continued, not waiting for a reply "you, ya gobshite, what the hell was all that about yesterday? I've seen you drinking here for a while and you've barely said ten words, what did Paul ever do to wind you up so much?" Padraig took a deep breath and tried to remember the speech he'd written while supposedly working overnight. He began;

"Charlie, I …um… just wanted to, you know, mmm… apologise for what happened yesterday. This is my favourite pub in the town and …. mmm …… you've always treated me well and I don't want to have to find… to find somewhere else to drink."

Charlie eventually put the poor sod out of his misery. "Ah will you relax for fucks sake, you're not in court. You had raised words in a pub, no punches thrown, no physical contact and you left when asked."

"Thanks to me!" Derek pointed out, beaming with pride.

"Shut the fuck up you and go over and lose some money on the fruit machine. Listen …. Mmm…?"

"Padraig" he said

"Yeah Padraig, that's it. Listen Padraig as far as I'm concerned that part of it is over and done with and behind us all. However is there another issue you wanted to apologise for?"

Padraig's cheeks reddened a touch for the first time in years. "Ah God I'm sorry, I did have a few choice words about you before we got in to it. I'm really sorry; can we just leave it as a bad day?" Padraig was on the point of breaking and Charlie knew it must've been very out of character for this to affect him so much.

"Listen up fella. If bar staff didn't have thick skins they wouldn't make it more than a week. Mix drink with some gobshites and you get called all sorts of names.

That goes double for any woman behind a counter. We
have to fight hard to get the respect barmen get instantly.
But if you cross a line I'll find the strength to throw you
out on your arse myself. We clear?"

"Crystal"

"Right two things to say. Number one, Paul will be in
during the week and definitely next Sunday again. First
thing you do is apologise when you see him. Second
what did you walk in here to drink?"

"Pint of stout please Charlie, thanks for understanding."

"Right what's done is done. I'll put your pint on but I've
just thought of one more thing. Don't be drinking down
here with the dregs of the town. Would you get yourself
up to the top of the pub and we'll look after you up
there?"

5.

"It would be a great morning for the tide to be out wouldn't it old friend? I'm having a horrible morning and I'm in need of a long walk to blow the cobwebs off." Paul looked down at Rusty as he pulled the gate closed behind him. The poor fella hadn't many long walks left in him but he'd helped him through so many dark times. Even still it was asking a bit much, even for Rusty, to expect him to answer back now after all these years.
Paul had slipped out of bed around 6.30 am. He'd barely slept at all and he didn't want his tossing and turning to keep Maura from sleeping any longer. He slid out of bed and tip-toed down the stairs. Years of coming in drunk after last call had taught him every creaking floorboard from the hall door to his side of the bed. Now all he had to do was work in reverse.
He also knew not to try and close the bedroom door. Its' creaking hinges had given him away a few times before. As he crossed the landing to the top of the stairs Paul noticed that both Jack's and Louise's bedroom doors were closed tight. 'Jack's job mustn't be starting this week and is Louise going to be taking another Monday morning off school?' Paul thought 'more money down the drain.'
Switching off the alarm Paul reached for his house keys off the hook in the hall. 'I'm so tired but I won't be sleeping anymore tonight. Why did you let that young fella in the pub get under your skin so easily yesterday? I mean it's not like he was having a go at you personally, come on let's get the coffee on.'

Paul pushed the button on the coffee machine and heard it begin to bubble away. Opening the back door, Paul whispered quietly for Rusty. He needn't have bothered; his faithful friend knew the score when Paul was having an early start. Rusty walked slowly from his kennel and into the kitchen. As Paul looked down at his collie, he wondered was his slow walk because of the routine or was he finally beginning to show signs of his advanced years.

As the coffee maker continued to do its job, Paul went in to the front room to pick up his paper. Bringing it back to the kitchen table he fed Rusty his crusts off the table, the way he never did when Maura was about. Sitting down with a steaming coffee Paul wanted to read the paper, the one he hadn't read any of yesterday. Normally Paul would spend his Sunday afternoons dozing on and off and flicking through the paper. Yesterday he had dozed on and off but that had more to do with the pints than any relaxation he was feeling.

Even going through the newspaper was proving a tough ask for Paul this morning. Concentration was beyond him and he kept reading and re-reading the same stories. Before long he gave up and sat staring at the kitchen wall.

Memories stared back at Paul from that very same wall. There were photos of himself and Maura on honeymoon, holiday snaps of the four of them around Ireland and abroad. Photos of school graduations and family weddings. 'There must be 30 photos in that collage' Paul thought 'but it's the ones that are missing that are talking to me this morning.'

Without realizing it Paul whiled away an hour or so staring at the wall and ignoring the rest of his pot of coffee. "Right Rusty, we're out of here. If we don't leave now we'll never be back to the Church to meet Maura for 10 o'clock."

Maura heard Paul as he left the house. Despite his best efforts the lock had gone very fiddly lately and there was always a rattle going out or coming in the door. She listened carefully as Paul closed the gate behind him. Maura waited, she wanted to make sure Paul hadn't forgotten anything and wouldn't be coming back into the house.

Eventually she got out of bed and headed for the kitchen. She pulled her dressing gown off the back of the bedroom door and slipped it on as she went down the stairs. She stopped at the bottom of the stairs and looked at the photos of her 2 children on their various special days. The innocence and beauty of their smiling faces contrasted starkly with the hassled look and forced smiles on both Paul's face and hers. He'd made it to most events, big or small, unlike some parents but as she looked at the photos she realised he had been there in body but not necessarily in mind.

"Is Dad gone?" Jack asked as he ran across the landing heading for his half hour long shower.

"Yes love, he's just left with Rusty for his walk now."

"About time, I've been playing on my phone for an hour waiting for him to leave! He was in strange form yesterday wasn't he?"

Maura was about to reply when she heard the lock on the bathroom door. Jack wasn't asking a question, he knew and Maura knew and even Louise knew he'd been in odd form. Truth was he was acting as strangely subdued as any of them had seen him.

Carrying on into the kitchen, Maura filled and boiled the kettle for her first cup of the day, the first of many. As she did so, she lit a cigarette, one of many today she hoped but definitely not her first. Almost as soon as Paul had left the bed this morning she'd begun to smoke out the window at the front of the house.

Maura had started smoking 24 years ago in 1990, stopped 21 years ago but was making her way through the emergency box she kept in her jewellery box. Maura sipped her tea, took a long drag on her cigarette and settled in. She wanted to make sense of Paul's behaviour yesterday but that wouldn't be a quick or easy task.

"Bloody hell Mam, are you back on those cancer sticks? I haven't seen you smoke those since Nana died." Louise entered the kitchen with a flick of her coiffured hair. She liked making an entrance and Maura presumed that was why she announced her arrival with perfume and pheromones.

"What does this morning make it? 4 Monday mornings missed in a row? God forbid you'd put the opportunity to learn something before the Leaving Cert somewhere near the top of your list of priorities."

"Listen Mam, I don't need to go in there to let Professor Chalking perv on me and show us all his arousal through his chalk dusted trousers, he must be the only teacher in the world still using a blackboard."

"Yes but…"

"Yes but nothing Mam. He is a proper creep and I have Brendan picking up my notes. Anyway back to more important things. Will you stub out that cigarette? In years to come you can smoke yourself to oblivion if you want but while me and Golden Boy live under this roof can you leave it out?"

"Yeah okay love, you're right" Maura agreed while stubbing out her cigarette. "Is he really that bad that teacher you have on Mondays? Maybe you're doing the right thing but I just want you to use the brains you have to match your beauty. Just do yourself a favour and make sure you've a degree to your name after 4 years in college?"

"Will do Mam," Louise grabbed an apple heading for the door, "Brains are why I showered last night to avoid their lordships, senior and junior this morning and beauty? Well beauty comes from an apple a day, oh and not smoking!" Louise smiled back at her Mam as she pulled the door closed before adding "don't go lighting another one now I'm gone, I'm messaging Jack to watch out for you smoking again."

Maura was overcome with pride at her daughter and how she had turned out and Jack too. Somehow, despite it all, they'd two wonderful children, full of confidence but lacking in ego. Their children had at times raised themselves. Paul had thrown himself into his work. He never left them wanting for anything except maybe their emotional needs. Maura knew she was as guilty at times over the years. In spending so much time trying to get Paul to engage she hadn't been present for all their needs either. More than Paul yes but that wasn't hard and she knew she should have done more. She almost cried as she whispered I love you after her youngest closed the hall door.

"Put the cigarette out and nobody needs to get hurt. This is the cancer police and we don't want to smell anything in that kitchen!"

"Don't worry son, your sister got there before you and despite what she may have text you, I haven't lit another one since she left."

"Good Mam because we need you for years and years still." Tears poured forth from Maura's stressed, tired and emotional head.

"I love you son, you know that don't you? I'm sorry we weren't there for you and Louise more."

"Hey, hey, hey, steady on there Mam, what's with the water works? The 'change' starting already for you?" Jack was teasing but he knew it was his best weapon to bring her back to herself. "Listen to me, turn up your hearing aid and listen." He said holding her tight in his arms. "We give out about you and Dad but you did great and don't tell Louise I said this but as sisters go, she could be worse. Dad was in odd form yesterday but by the time he gets back from his walk, he'll have moved on. So march yourself upstairs and get ready for Mass. We can't have Fr. Murphy seeing you arriving late with tears in your eyes."

As Maura rose from the table she kissed her son's forehead. "You're a fine boy; you always know what to say." She wiped the tears from her eyes and headed for the stairs. By the time she was halfway up. Jack was heading for the front door.

"Oh Mam?"

"Yes son, what is it?" she asked turning towards him, her eyes still moist.

"Will you text me if Dad's still in shite form after his walk?"

"I will J, that's very thoughtful"

"It's not for his benefit, it's for mine. If he is still in shite form I can stay on for another 20 frames with Danny!" With that he was gone with the sound of the slammed door ringing in Maura's ears. Maura turned and walked to her room shaking her head. 'He's a lovely boy but that cheeky, mischievous nature of his is Paul all over at that age.' Maura burst into tears once again thinking of all the other things that weren't the same as they used to be when she and Paul began dating.

6.

Staring at the old man in the mirror, Paul didn't like
what he saw. Having walked the legs off himself and
Rusty along the harbour beach, he hoped to be feeling a
little better and in better control of his emotions. The
fresh air had done him a little good and he felt a little
refreshed when he returned home with Maura after Mass.
She had tried a couple of times to bring him into
conversation but he had resisted all her efforts. Even in
his best form he was never a fan of conversation, so after
being unsuccessful a couple of times, Maura had given
up and left him to his silence all evening. A bath and
watching the soaps had taken up most of the evening
while Paul sat, staring mutely at characters and storylines
he didn't know.

As Paul looked at himself from head to toe in the mirror
he tried to see the young father he had been 24 years ago.
The echoes of that man could just about be seen but he
had long since lost his youthful looks and enthusiasm.
That tragic evening was etched into the weary lines on
his forehead. His eyes were hollow and drawn and there
was no light or spark in his eye.

Thinking of James, Paul opened his wallet to look upon
his eldest boy once more. He was never far from his
thoughts but Paul still liked to look into his 3 year old
sons' eyes and remember a time before their lives were
changed so tragically. Opening the back credit card slots
of his wallet he longed to see his curly-haired little boy
looking back at him. But with rising panic, Paul opened,
closed and re-opened the wallet hoping that somehow it

was just a cruel trick that he hadn't seen it the first few times.

Beads of cold sweat formed on his neck as he searched in vain for the photo. 'What's happened? Where the fuck is it?' he thought. Paul slammed his keys and phone on to the chest of drawers and turned and fired the wallet across the room. "What a useless piece of shit! I can't believe you've lost my photo of James!" Paul was screaming at his wallet. Hoping beyond hope the inanimate object would apologise for the ruse and return the photo to its' rightful spot. Paul picked up the wallet and opened it slowly, praying like he hadn't for at least twenty years. Paul had no luck and flung it across the bedroom once more.

Maura entered the room and nearly took a wallet to the face for her troubles. "I was coming to ask what you were slamming and stomping about for but I nearly got a close-up didn't I? What were you trying to do? Did you figure out you spent more than you expected down The Local?" But on this occasion she was so wrong.

"That fucking wallet has gone and lost my photo of James. The one and only photo I kept of him. I've nothing else to remember him by. I don't know where I'm after losing it and there isn't another around the house and there's no chance of getting another one to replace it and there's......."

"Wait Paul, wait, will you? Yes it's awful that you've lost your photo of James but he's still with us all the time. I've the box of old photos in the attic under the Christmas decorations. We can go up and get you a replacement from there when the kids are out tomorrow, can't we?"

"It won't be the same photo though will it? It won't be the one of him and me in Castle Park when he was at his happiest will it? There's a reason I held on to that photo above all others. And I know we agreed not to tell Louise and Jack about James but this last week has brought it all back to me and now losing the photo just adds to that you know?"

"I do Paul, I do. Remember, I'm the only other person who knows what we're going through."

"But it isn't WE Maura is it? You don't know the guilt and sadness I carry with me and how much happiness I get from looking at those soft blonde curls of his."

"Don't be boxing me out again Paul, it is WE, WE decided not to tell the kids, WE decided to deal with this ourselves and WE are the ones living with the sorrow and the broken hearts." Maura lost herself in deep sobbing and collapsed to the bed as if the wind had been punched clean out of her. Exactly how she had felt all those years ago.

"It's just with little Patricia's funeral, the little white coffin and everything, I've been staring at the photograph more and more this week. Jaysus wept, every time I looked at it I could smell the fresh cut grass, could feel the sunshine and the sun cream lathered on to him the evening that photo was taken. I hated taking photographs and hated being in them even more so why did I ask that man to take our photo that day? What compelled me to take that step? Was it a premonition and did someone plan it out that way? And don't start on about Gods' plan Maura, you know it's all bullshit in my mind."

Maura hadn't even had a chance to think it, never mind say it before Paul had cut her off. She knew her faith was not something that Paul understood or found comfort in at any point in the last 24 years.

"I know you've found some comfort in scripture and Church going but I can't believe it was planned by some higher power to take our little lad away, I mean how could there be someone so cruel?"

Maura wouldn't allow herself to think that way, ever. She had tried desperately to find the reason behind their loss and even though that hadn't become clear just yet, she had to believe, had to, that there was a higher purpose for little James.

"Have you been beating yourself up again this week Paul? Nothing good can come of that and you know it"

"I know, I know" Paul agreed, "but it's been hard not to be to be honest. I mean the echoes are all there this past while with what has happened to Brian O'Neill. I wouldn't be human if I didn't hear them. I mean for fucks sake he was the one supposed to be looking after her like I should've been doing for James. It can happen so quickly and he must be tying himself in knots with the guilt."

By this point Paul had sat himself on the end of the bed beside Maura and she could see his massive guilt-filled tears plummeting from his face again. She moved towards him and gently manoeuvred herself under his arm and held him close.

"There was absolutely nothing you could have done Paul, nothing at all. It's an awful, terrible state of affairs but accidents can and do happen. They can and do happen." She was repeating this last sentence into his ear

as they rocked backwards and forwards together in an
embrace and closeness they hadn't felt in years.
"Accidents can and do happen Paul, they can and do
happen."
"Except they never happened on your watch did they
love?"

7.

"You can't be serious! He's got to be ok; he's just got to be!" Paul couldn't accept that his son was in a dangerous position and might not make it through the night. What had begun as a quick and thoughtful father/son evening out had turned into a nightmare Paul would struggle to wake from for a quarter of a century.

The sun was shining brilliantly on June 11th, 1990, it was high, it was bright and it was warm. The country was gripped by World Cup fever and there was optimism in the people of Ireland not seen since the Pope's visit in 1979. The Irish people felt invincible and there was an opportunity to beat the English too, which always felt a bit special.

Paul Forsyth was no football man and had absolutely no intention of joining the millions of people who were planning on spending their evening watching the match. As he drove the short distance from his office to home he was thinking of what he could do. From nowhere he had an idea of taking James to Castle Park for a go on the swings. If other fathers and sons would be bonding watching a football match, he could do the same with his beautiful boy.

As he continued along his journey Paul had another thought. His son was now over three years old and yet he'd never once told him that he thought he was beautiful or that he loved him. Paul knew it was there and he told everyone else he loved his son but as an Irish man he found verbalizing his love for his son very difficult. Instead he showed his love by holding James as much as possible and providing everything he could ever want or need.

Maura had noticed, as she always did, that Paul struggled to tell his son he loved him. Indeed she was used to that herself as it wasn't until their wedding day that Paul had looked her in her eye, held her hand and told her from the bottom of his heart that he loved her with all his being. She'd known it and she knew he loved James but it would still be nice to hear Paul say it.

So when Paul arrived in from work and announced he was taking James to the park, Maura saw an opportunity to remind Paul of what he already knew. "You'll be all by yourselves up there. Everyone else is going to be in watching the football so take the opportunity to tell him. I know you love him but it'd be nice for you say it out loud and once you do it once, you won't feel any embarrassment in the future."

As the car made its way towards the Park, James began to recognise the road and was telling Paul which way to turn to get to the car park and then to the playground. As a new father Paul had no clue what it was James wanted or needed before he learned to speak. But now James was full of chat and had no problem telling Paul exactly what he wanted. As they drove the winding road from the gate to the car park, Paul kept his eyes in the rear view mirror watching James take in everything around them, his eyes darting from one side window to the other. Then there was an explosion of pure joy on his face and he let out a little squeal of delight as he spotted the playground. "Over there Daddy, over there!"

"I know son, I know it is but you can't take off your belt until I've stopped the car." James wasn't listening though and was out of his car seat and standing on the back of Pauls' belt before he knew it.

"James you're choking me! Stop your messing and get back in your seat!" Having got a shock from the belt choking him and seeing James out of his seat, Paul was shouting at his little boy. In an instant James' excitement disappeared from his face, he slunk back into his booster seat and his bottom lip began to curl. All Pauls' good intentions were gone to hell and when he had the car parked, he took off the damn seat belt and turned to face his bawling child.

"I'm sorry for shouting James but you gave Daddy a fright and I didn't want you getting hurt by being loose in the back seat. I didn't mean to shout, I'm really sorry son."

James' bottom lip was still curled and he was crying huge sobs of fright and anger. 'This will take some recovery Pauly boy' he thought to himself as he went to the back doors to let James out.

"Come on and we'll have a go in the playground..... or we can go the farm and look at the pigs if you wanted?" Success thought Paul as James stopped crying. His face did a miraculous transformation and suddenly he was back to Pauls' smiling, chatty blonde haired boy.

"I love the pigs Dad, they make funny noises" James was giggling to himself "and they smell funny too!"

"Is it a bad smell?"

"No it's a good smell but it smells really bad.... but, but I like it smelling bad. It smells like the farm."

"Oh I see" Paul said, noticing how much easier it was that James could use words to explain his thinking.

They only stayed at the farm for a few minutes before James got bored and wanted to have a go on the swings. Thinking back today, Paul can still remember exactly what his thoughts were in June 1990.

Standing on the path watching James walking along the fence feeding straw and grass through the fence to the pigs, Paul had a thought. 'Take your time and make sure to take advantage of days like today mate. Your son isn't going to be a little boy forever and he'll be too cool to hang out with you in his teens. Make sure you store away the memories of days like this and do it more often too.'

As he stood watching James pretend to be a farmer, Paul took a seat and noticed something in the pocket of his cargo shorts. Taking the object out he realised it was a disposable camera from the last sunny day, probably the year before. He'd never have brought a camera with him but now he'd found it he was curious as to what might be on the camera. A man walked past with his dog and Paul found himself asking him to take a photo of the two of them to finish off the roll.

Paul called James over to himself, to get in the frame as the man positioned himself to take the shot. Over 24 years Paul thought back to that moment in front of the pigs on regular occasions. Why had he done something so out of character in asking the man to take the photograph? He had never gotten to the point of believing he had pre-meditated the harrowing events about to unfold and needed a memento. If that was true then he would've felt even more guilt than he did anyway for not protecting his boy.

Instead his belief was that something or someone had let him know how important those memories would be and he'd been guided to bringing James to the park on his own and then to step out of his comfort zone to get their photograph taken. It was an odd feeling and sensation that he had had some sense of foreboding take over his actions since he left work that evening.

Later that night, over the next year and on numerous occasions over the last quarter of a century Paul had been so grateful to that sense of foreboding. It had allowed him one last evening with his boy and given him a precious photograph by which to remember James' short life.

Those memories and thoughts can be comforting but they also brought so many negative thoughts and emotions. 'If I hadn't felt like I had to bring James alone, would Maura have been with us? If after getting the photograph taken we were happy, then why hadn't we gone straight home? What if they had never gone to the playground? What if? What if? What if?'

As grateful as Paul is to have had that photograph in his wallet all these years, now that it was gone he found his emotions back in the days following James' death. Feeling the same guilt, the same shame and the same anger he had held in check for so many years. As Maura held him, rocking back and forth on their marital bed, it was these feelings as much as loss and sadness that drew the tears from his eyes. Guilt, shame and anger; the Holy Trinity of grieving emotions.

8.

James had been knocked down and life would never be the same again. It wasn't a sound Paul had ever heard before but instantly he knew what he'd heard and that that sound would haunt him for the rest of his life. Of course he had no certainty but the sound he heard left little room for doubt.

"Push me higher Dad, push me higher!" James was flying high on the swings. Feeling safe and comfortable with his Dad he was a little braver.

"Just a little bit higher now son." These swings aren't really built for brave boys like you who want to go really high." Paul smiled as James' laughter and excitement got higher and higher until he was gasping for air. Paul was happier and more relaxed than he had been in days; playing with his son, enjoying the sunshine and forgetting about the stresses and strains of work.

For a second time since arriving in Castle Park, Paul heard and listened to a little voice inside his head.

'You've got to remember the days like today and take stock of the little details rather than being overcome by the broader world. Take in the clear blue sky, the bright sunshine, the green trees and your sons' smile. Not to mention James' nervous little giggle he gave as he reached the top of his arc on the swings.'

"Dad? Dad? I'm slowing down, you have to push me!" James interrupted his Dad and brought him back to the present.

"Sorry young man, I was away with the fairies."

"You like fairies Dad? Uhhh that's girl stuff!" James was making no effort to hide the disgust in his voice at what his Dad had said.

"It's just a saying son. I was kind of dreaming even though I was awake."

"That's weird Dad, I don't want you to like fairies"

"Ok, ok I won't say it again I promise." Paul was laughing to himself at how head strong James was but he didn't want to laugh out loud in case his son thought he was laughing at him. Instead he suggested they head for home. "Come on so, we'll go home and maybe Mammy will get you something nice for being a good boy." Paul said this as he lifted James down from the swing and James was off like a shot as soon as his feet hit the ground. The quicker he got to the car, the quicker he'd get his ice-cream, he thought.

"Hang on, hang on James, I've to get your sun hat and hoodie from the see-saw." He'd put them in to avoid a row with Maura as they were leaving. It was sunny and warm as they left but Maura was afraid it would get too cold if the sun went down or that James would burn if he didn't wear his hat. She was always over worrying and second guessing herself. "James hang, on, wait for me!" Paul was calling over his shoulder as he went to get the hat and jumper.

But James was off to the races.

Like lightning he was at the edge of the playground. He was already halfway back to the car. He was sprinting as fast as his little legs could carry him. Paul snatched the jumper and turned to run after James. He was sprinting now, trying desperately to catch his future Olympian. The world was speeding up and Paul felt he was running in treacle. He couldn't close the gap and the heat was suddenly oppressive for Paul.

James was out of Paul's sight now but heading in the right direction. They'd have some ice-cream when they got home, they'd tell Maura about the fairies, they'd have the photograph to look back on, they'd do this, they'd do that………..

Paul didn't see James smash the back of his head off the kerb after running into the tree. He heard it though. He heard the dull, heavy smack of concrete as James' head hit the path. He heard it deep down in the pit of his stomach. He knew instantly that his son was in trouble but he presumed he'd be alright. He rounded the corner to see his son lying on his back with his head resting awkwardly on the kerb. 'Kids bang their heads all the time. Come on James, get up son.' Paul was desperate as he approached his injured lad.

****

Twelve hours later Paul and Maura returned to their cold, empty house. It was mid-June but the temperature felt more like mid-December. Things had changed terribly since last night and life was never going to be the same again.

Maura made immediately for the kettle. It was 7 in the morning, she was exhausted but the idea of closing her eyes and maybe having to accept the horrible truth was terrifying her. Paul merely stood in the door jamb – numb, unmoving and undoubtedly in shock his legs would take him no further. He felt his shoulders hunched over and he had aged 10 years overnight.

"Have a cuppa Paul and sit down with me." Maura wasn't asking, she was telling. She was in shock herself but she felt she had to talk about her sons' death. 'Oh Holy God' she thought to herself 'my son is dead. It's not supposed to be like this. What did he ever do to deserve that? What did we ever do to deserve that?' Maura had to literally take Paul by the hand and guide him to the kitchen table. "I can't believe he's gone" was what he kept repeating. "One second he's here and the next he is gone."

"That's what we've got to hold on to love, he felt no pain. Remember what the doctor said, he was gone as soon as he caught his head on the kerb."

"No pain Maura? No fucking pain?" Paul was shouting now, "How could he not have felt pain with a fractured skull and…. Good God he is only 3 years old, the only pain he should have is from catching his shins on the table."

"Was 3 Paul, he was" Maura had mumbled instinctively and she would never know why.

"What did you say Maura? Was? For fucks sake woman our son died overnight and you're already talking in the past tense! I can't cope with this." Paul pushed back his chair, slamming his palms on the table as he did so. "I can't talk to you if you're going to be like this!"

Maura moved her hand to try and grab hold of Pauls' arm. "Don't block me out love. We need to work together on this. I'm in shock too but we've got to find a way of moving forward and accepting what has happened."

Maura had always been a very practical woman. It was part of the reason Paul had fallen for her. She never got too up or too down in any situation but right this minute, that same practicality was winding him up like a caged bear being poked with a stick.

"You've obviously processed this already Maura but I can't. I keep replaying the moments in my mind and every time I see him get up and walk over to me. Then I'm hit by the grief and loss all over again every single time."

"I haven't processed it at all. How could I? I feel as sad, as angry and as lost as you are but we've got to start dealing with this situation in some way."

"This situation Maura? It's not like somebody lost a job. Our son is DEAD!" Paul was right in Maura's' face now and roaring at her. Anger, sadness and frustration were all visible on his face.

"Do you think I don't know that?" she roared back. "But I've got to keep busy, got to DO something to distract my mind from the awful truth."

"I just can't do that yet Maura and I definitely can't talk about James in the past tense. It's just too soon."

"It might be too soon, but we've got to do these things at some stage so why not now?"

"Because I'm not ready and I'm afraid I'll say something I'll regret."

"Say something you'll regret? What could you possibly say that you'd regret?"

Paul had been backing away through the latest exchange and so stopped with one hand on the bannister and his left foot on the first step. Despite the intense anger and hurt he was feeling he delivered his next line slowly, deliberately and in a hushed whisper.

"It's your fault Maura" he began "if you hadn't insisted on me bringing his jumper and a fucking hat on a summers' evening; I wouldn't have had to go back for them and I'd have been with James and stopped him from running."

Paul trudged up the stairs to a sleepless, tear-filled few hours of waking nightmares. Meanwhile in the kitchen Maura cursed Paul and his vicious tongue and she cursed God for taking away her pride and joy. She collapsed on to her arms and cried and cried and cried.

Maura was crying so hard, she felt her heart would actually break down under the strain. As she sat at the kitchen table she eventually let out a high-pitched, guttural shriek "why God?! Why have you chosen to put this awful tragedy on us?! We've always being good and done right so why have you left us now?!"

9.

"It's all going to be ok. You are here in a safe place, we will acknowledge your pain and sadness and we will allow you to appreciate the gift of life your little boy was and how you were blessed with his time here. However brief it may have been."

Bereavement counsellor Suzy, definitely not Susie, was in full flow. Paul and Maura had entered her rooms at least five, if not 10, minutes ago. They were yet to say more than hello, themselves. Suzy had launched into a pre-learned spiel she gave to all new clients. Her voice altered between a sky-high child of the seventies and the voiceover artist used on hypnosis tapes.

"What was his name?" Paul asked suddenly, remembering the location of his vocal chords. "We may as well not have been here for the first section of this one woman show. That's the real reason I interrupted, just to remind you we are here."

"You've both experienced a sudden and incredible loss and we will spend the coming weeks dealing with and hopefully accepting the challenge you've been set."

"Our son died less than a month ago and we are still incredibly raw."

"I can assure you I'm well aware of your family background and we will aim to take the next steps together and improve the quality of life you have at the moment."

"It's Sean" Paul replied, simultaneously squeezing Maura's hand hoping she wouldn't contradict him straight away. But Paul needn't have worried, Maura stayed quiet long enough for the counsellor to trip herself up.

"Sean, of course it is, little Sean Forsyth. I do hear a lot of stories so I can get mixed up but I remember now. I talked through the illness that Sean had with our director so that I could learn all about it."

The words were left hanging in mid-air, barely out of Suzy's mouth. Paul tapped Maura's hand gently, stood up and said "let's go love; we're not going to get any of the help we might need here."

Suzy was taken aback by the sudden twist the session had taken. She wracked her brain trying to find the section in the text books that would help her regain control of the situation. "I know this concept can seem a little alien to you both and I'm sorry I forgot Sean's name, but in time you'll realise the vital role this time will be in allowing you to grieve and maybe even find a way to move forward."

Paul ignored her completely and continued delicately helping Maura put her coat on. He held it behind her back as she slipped it on and then placed a comforting hand between her shoulder blades. He began to guide her towards the door, something he hadn't done for far too long.

"Thanks love," Maura said as she made for the door "you were right about all this being rubbish. Maybe we will be better dealing with this alone?"

"I know this process can be odd for people and it's not for everyone but I've never had a couple give up on the process so quickly." Suzy didn't add that she'd never had a couple in with her alone before. "But to refer to my profession as rubbish I find very insulting."

Maura didn't hesitate but rather continued her progress towards the door. Paul hadn't spoken but his mind was racing to come up with the most suitable retort. As he turned to close the office door behind them, the words shot in to his mind.

"If you weren't such a false and insincere person scrounging money off the vulnerable you might find a career in this. Although your words seem compassionate, your condescension and lack of respect is what comes across. We DO need to be supported and helped and considered but not by someone pretending to care and only thinking of the bottom line."

Paul left his final sentence until the last possible second before the door closed. "We all know you couldn't possibly have prepared properly for our meeting. Because if you had done anything you'd know our son's name is James and he died in an accident and not of any illness."

****

The kettle had boiled a long time ago and Paul was simply letting the water cool behind him. They had made their way home from the clinic arm in arm. It was the first time in over a month they had touched in any intimate way. Their closeness felt both physical and mental. The physical strain of losing their only son was something they both could relate to. They had however been in different places mentally with regard to how much of a toll they had borne.

Paul blamed himself and felt incredibly guilty about his role in the accident. He spent his days thinking of what he could have done differently while Maura was more influenced by the gaping hole in their here and now. She got upset at every new reminder of James' absence. The mornings she slept past his normal waking time, she wondered why he hadn't run in and jumped on her bed. Each time was another reminder of what he'd never do again.

Paul wasn't keen on the idea of grief counselling and resented being told that talking about his emotions would help. Maura, however, was enthusiastic to give anything a go if it might reduce their pain and suffering. As was always the case, Maura had won that conversation. They would at least give it a try and decide if that kind of treatment would be good for them.

So when Paul had given Suzy the wrong name and she had believed him and continued lying, they were suddenly on the same page. Nobody could understand what they were going through by reading books. Only those who'd walked a mile in their shoes could help. Strolling home arm in arm, sharing their strength and moving as one for the first time in many months they felt strong and united. Paul had hung his coat on the rack before turning to help Maura with hers. He had then made for the kitchen and suggested a cup of tea. The same cup of tea Maura was still waiting on as the water continued to cool behind Paul's back.

"Paul I'm so glad that we're actually talking and sharing with each other and the help you gave me on and off with my coat is a small thing but it means a lot to me. But if I could say all this while sipping on a cuppa I'd be twice as happy!"

"Jaysus Maura of course, of course, I just got lost there for a minute, one cup of rosy lee on the way." Paul flicked the switch and moved towards Maura and took her hands in his. He helped her to stand and maintaining eye contact throughout, spoke directly to her.

"I've no idea what will help us get over our loss love, or if we ever will at all. But know this, I'll be here and we'll do it together. It might have to be me and you against the world but we'll get there. It certainly won't involve any namby-pamby, hippy shite about growth and acceptance from Suzy with a Z. You go ahead in to the sitting room and I'll follow in with the tea. I might even get the fancy jug out that you like to use even when it's just us."

"You know you might be right Paul. I'm so disappointed and upset because I thought grief counselling as a couple could really help us." Maura felt the tears in the corner of her eyes and held Paul tight, enjoying the support and strength he provided her. "Kettle's boiled again love!" she whispered in his ear before kissing his cheek and moving down the hall.

"Jaysus Christ I'll burn out the feckin element at this rate."

Just then the phone rang on the hall table. "I've got it" Maura said and pulled the door behind her. "041-6857171.......... oh hello Suzy......... I didn't expect you to call us so soon........"

Paul heard Maura's side of the conversation begin and he did feel a little bit of respect for Suzy ringing to apologise but he knew after the conversation with Maura in the kitchen, Suzy was wasting her time. He turned his attention back to the teapot and the jug and putting the biscuits on to a plate, all the little unnecessary stuff that Maura liked to do.

10.

"Each and every first is going to be incredibly hard to get through. The first birthday, the first Christmas, all of those events will remind you of the loved one you've lost. But we hope that having come together as a support network for each other that when you do think of them, you remember the good times and memories and they aren't solely reminders of the pain and sadness."

On a bitter cold night three weeks before Christmas, with the Parish Hall heating at its' default setting of broken down, Suzy was laying it on the line for the group of bereaved parents. It was true that Christmas would naturally stir up emotions but in time it wouldn't always be sadness and loss that was evoked.

Maura gazed around the circle as Suzy spoke. Everyone was crying and they all dabbed absent-mindedly at the corners of their eyes. But underneath the sadness Maura noticed something else. Those in the group who had lost a child a number of years before were nodding along with Suzy. They were overtly ignoring their tears and agreeing with her that things could get better. They seemed to be saying that grief would indeed not always be the first emotion evoked when she thought of James. The group had obviously helped them massively

In the six months since Maura visited Suzy alone for the first time, she hadn't been able to coax Paul into coming with her but at Suzy's suggestion she had begun to visit the bereavement group as well as seeing Suzy individually. Paul still vehemently felt that James' death was so awful that no God would've let it happen. His mind wasn't for changing and he said to Maura that he didn't like the links between Suzy, the Priest, the Parish and the community. He felt they should be separate but they were all linked together.

Maura, meanwhile, had trusted in God implicitly since she was old enough to make her own decisions on such matters. She had believed in the greater good. She had believed in heaven and she had believed in an all-knowing God who would lead her on her life's path. She had believed in this, she had trusted in this and she had accepted this when she faced challenges to be overcome in life. She had done all of these things.

These last few weeks however, she'd begun to question some of the beliefs she had held fast to for many years. Suzy could never give a straight answer to her questions about life and death. She also delivered every word she spoke in a soothing monotone voice obviously learnt from some evening course she had attended. In their individual sessions Suzy discussed everything and anything but in the group setting her whole delivery and outlook seemed different. Maura couldn't understand it at first but had spent many hours thinking about it. So much so that she began to question what was being said in the Parish Hall with new vigour. Another surprising source, namely Paul, had also pushed her to question some things about her beliefs.

He hadn't wanted to be a part of that form of therapy but, after Maura had explained why she was continuing to see Suzy, he knew it could benefit her. He asked her when she might begin to feel better and start to recover after all the talking, crying, praying she'd done and Maura couldn't find an answer. He asked what actual difference was there between him going to the pub and her going to a draughty hall to talk and talk. And she couldn't answer. He asked her did she continue to trust and believe in God and his over-arching plan. And she couldn't answer.

The questions around her faith and the time she spent in prayer to God troubled her. She had always been a practising Catholic and that was it. But now where did she stand? She still believed in Him but she no longer believed that her faith was the only way for her to deal with her grief. She no longer held fast to prayer and discussion could manage her grief in isolation. She began to think that, in an odd way, maybe Paul had been correct all along?

He had disassociated himself from the church and God as soon as James died and while Maura wasn't ready for such a drastic measure, she was still being forced to think about questions she had never conceived would be part of her life. Had Paul in his angry, cranky way followed the more correct path.

****

"What time do you make it now love?" Maura looked disconsolately at her watch before answering Paul. "It's only just gone two o'clock."

"Two o'clock? Ah for jaysus sake this day is going to last forever. We haven't even had a chance to miss the Queen's speech yet!"

Paul was disgusted and utterly dejected. December 25th 1990 was making a home for itself as the second longest day of his life. Second only to June 11th 1990. Paul shifted in himself a little and re-settled against the arm of the couch. Once he stopped moving, Maura repositioned herself against his large frame, so he could continue to hold her and try to somehow shield her from the worst of the emotional onslaught.

They had risen at half seven in the morning. They had risen and not awoken. Sleep had been impossible and they had suffered the awful sound of complete silence overnight. James hadn't fallen asleep vowing to stay awake and meet Santa Claus, he hadn't stirred from time to time to check his stocking. He hadn't gotten sick through the whole excitement and magic of Christmas. Instead Paul and Maura had done the tossing and turning. They had tried, ultimately in vain, to sleep off the slab of beer and two bottles of wine they'd put away Christmas Eve. But sleep eluded them all night before they eventually roused themselves to get showered and set for the day.

Showering, dressing, breakfasting and leaving the house were all done in silence. Not a word shared between them, not a kiss or hug for that matter. Instead they made the slow stroll towards the church, walking so slowly they hoped they'd never actually get there. Paul might not believe too strongly any more but Christmas Day was different.

Once inside the church and sitting again in the swollen pews, things got even tougher for the Forsyths. Some of the youngest children had a new toy with them and those that didn't were floating around with massive smiles on their faces, fuelled by happiness, wonder and probably too much sugar.

The parents were beaming with pride as they saw their cherubic children enjoying Christmas morning. Most of the youngsters were unaware they were at the church to celebrate the real meaning of Christmas. It was their parents' way of ensuring December 25th was primarily a religious celebration. Not to mention the fact that if they didn't show up at Mass, everyone else in the town would notice.

However once they saw their children moving towards Paul and Maura, pushing toy cars along the railings of the pews, they whisper shouted at their children to come back to their seats. They would then try to explain to very confused children why they weren't allowed to smile, play with their toys or run around that particular part of the church.

These same parents thought they were being supportive and mindful of Paul and Maura's loss but really they were compounding the sense of loss and disconnect they were experiencing. Stopping these innocent children from doing what children do only served to remind them that they would never again scold James over trivialities or feel his excitement on days of celebration. 'For jaysus sake, Paul would think to himself, these little ones don't need to suffer too.'

The final straw for Paul and Maura arrived when the Priest asked if the congregation could pray for all those who had suffered loss in the past year. In this still moment of reflection they sat hand in hand, staring at the floor through tearful eyes. All their loss distilled into 30 seconds of quiet. Paul prayed, like he hadn't for months, that the Priest would carry on quickly. But he wouldn't. In trying to show them that the community supported them, he instead forced them to hear the merciless silence as time stood still.

Paul and Maura never took their eyes of their respective spots on the floor but later that day they described to each other how they had felt every pair of eyes in the congregation boring into them. Though full of sympathy and sadness this meant nothing to them. Instead they imagined that, while sympathising, these parents were also thanking God it wasn't them who had lost their children. That they weren't the ones watching children play with Santa's gifts, that they weren't the ones going home to a house without lights or decoration, a house whose soul and vibrancy had been stolen.

****

Paul returned from the kitchen with a fresh can in one hand and the bottle of red wine in the other. As he passed the sitting room window he saw the children pass by on new bikes, skateboards and in-line roller blades. He set the drinks down on the coffee table and yanked the curtains closed.

"Are all the kids out on their bikes?" Maura asked. "I know Grainne couldn't wait to see Doireann riding her bike and what's her name O'Toole across the road stopped me the other day to tell me how much it was killing her that her little one had to wait until Christmas morning for hers! They just have no comprehension of how we might be feeling."

"They've just moved on love. Remember how quickly the visitors and the cooked dinners stopped arriving at our door? They all sympathised but then they went back to their normal lives. I don't blame them but they can't understand and hopefully they never will."

64

"But should we reply by just blocking it out and closing the curtains?"

"I think for today love, we can do everything and anything that we want to do and fuck the rest of them." Adding as a finished off his can into his glass, "anything we want Maura, like having a drink and eating a box of chocolates since 10 this morning."

They settled on the couch with their drinks at easy reach watching some awful film on the television. "The TV bosses probably don't expect too many people not to be eating, drinking and opening presents but we couldn't be the only ones not partaking in the festive cheer who'd want to watch something decent, could we?"

11.

"Thanks so much for coming back to see me Maura, I know you had a terrible first experience with your husband. I just wanted to take the opportunity to try and explain what will happen between us over the next sessions."

"To be honest Pam, it's taken a lot for me to even step back in here today. I've been so lost and upset since James' death that I'm open to giving anything a try, including giving counselling a second chance. It definitely won't work for Paul though; he will not be coming back.

"I wouldn't blame him for that at all Maura, I haven't heard as bad a session as that since I started training. Even counsellors may let their own emotions interfere with how they set about the session. Forgetting James' name was inexcusable and I don't want to leave you with the impression that was all counselling sessions have to offer."

Hoping desperately to make amends for their shambolic experience Suzy had rung the Forsyth home. If Paul had picked up the phone, she knew it would have been a fruitless venture but she could have at least consoled herself that she had tried to act. Fortunately for her, it was Maura who picked up the phone which gave Suzy the opportunity to at least apologise.

Although Maura knew how badly the session had gone, she wanted desperately to believe what her friends had told her. They had said that their experience was the exception and not representative of the services available. So when Suzy identified herself, Maura ignored the urge to slam the receiver down and instead sat down on the bottom step of the stairs in the hall. Something in the tone of her voice and the honesty that seemed to back up the words she spoke convinced Maura to try again.

So when Paul came out of the kitchen with the tea tray in hand, Maura had already replaced the receiver in the cradle. "What did she want?" Paul asked as they sat on the couches and he began to pour the tea. "It was Suzy, she wanted to apologise for what had happened and invite us to go back and see her again."

"I presume you told her where to get off love yeah? Jaysus if that's what counselling has to offer then they are just charlatans making off with people's money and we won't be going down that road again."

"I just told her I accepted that she was sorry and that was it. It took guts I suppose to make the call so I let her have her say without cutting her off straight away."

"Jaysus you've the patience of a saint love, I'd have hung up as soon I knew who it was on the phone, and I probably would've accompanied it with a few choice words too!"

"No doubt you would have done Paul but would it have helped? She made a mistake, she apologised, let's just leave it behind us now ok?"

"Not a bother to me at all," Paul said enthusiastically, "if I never have to speak about counselling again that'll be fantastic. Jaysus love you talk about needing help and what counselling can do for you but you're more resilient than you realise Maura. Now enjoy your tea."

****

The gentle vibration of her watch on her wrist reminded Pam that it was time to finish. She and Maura had spoken freely and openly for the full hour. They'd barely mentioned James or indeed the previous session, instead they'd simply talked. They shared stories and histories almost like two old school friends catching up.

"I'm sorry Maura but we're going to have to stop there for today. Our hour is up and I've another client in about 15 minutes. "

"Was that really an hour? That just flew by. We didn't really talk about James though did we? Is that not the whole point of me being here?"

"I suppose it is Maura, but, if you're open to it, we will definitely spend time talking about James and your emotions in greater detail over the next few weeks. I know you didn't get off to a good start but we can fix that and move on."

"Absolutely I'd love to come back, I don't know what it is Pam, maybe it's part of your training but there's definitely a certain way or quality you have that has put me more at ease and allows me to talk like I rarely do."

"Well I'm glad to hear it Maura and as we begin to learn about each other too, the trust will grow stronger and the hope is that we can discuss things here, which may be difficult, but that you don't feel you can talk about elsewhere. Will I put you in the diary for this time next week or when is the best time for you?"

"This is fine but do you work Mondays by any chance? Paul's always in the pub so around 7 or 8 would be perfect and I wouldn't have to explain to him about coming here."

"Well maybe in time that is something you might want to broach with Paul, or we can talk about, for the sake of your relationship? But that is a discussion for another time. Instead I'll put you in for 8 o'clock next Monday and we can start from there." Pam rose from her chair and Maura took her cue to move too. Slowly they made their way towards the door and Maura began to put on her coat. The difference between the two counsellors could not have been starker. She spoke with honesty and strength of character that Maura couldn't put her finger on. But she felt full trust in this woman and genuinely believed she could help her through this awful period in her life.

"Thanks very much Pam, it's a pity about what happened but I don't think Paul is ready to talk about his feelings and emotions, so it might be a blessing in disguise that I'll be coming back on my own. Thanks again and I'll see you next Monday."

"It's no problem at all and I'll see you then. Don't worry about Paul, everyone reaches the point where counselling can help at different stages but I know by you that you are ready and this will help."

With that Pam reached out a hand and touched Maura's shoulder. As she did, their eyes met for just a split second longer than normal. Maura could feel that Pam was telling her something in these gestures but she couldn't figure it out at all. Instead she simply nodded her head and turned for the door. The walk back in to the town was much easier for Maura. She felt relieved to be moving forward and she was content in the knowledge

that Pam was going to help her do just that. It was
nothing she had said but more a feeling she gave Maura
about the protection she could offer.

Maura stopped outside McHugh's butchers to check out
the offers when the realisation hit her. She knew what
Pam had been trying to say with her eyes. 'She knows
what I'm going through. She gets the degree of loss I've
had because she's had it too.' That's what Maura
realised and she knew that there hadn't been just one
woman remembering the loss of her son in the room but
two. Pam had felt the exact same pain.

She had said it can be a very feint line that exists
between counsellor and the client they meet with. In
order to get the very most from the sessions very often
they will discuss issues and emotions they haven't
discussed with anyone else. They may even discuss
issues they have been afraid to verbalise and so the trust
must be strong and true between them.

This is particularly true of someone detailing their
experience of loss and going through the grieving
process. Maura felt comfortable discussing everything
with Pam. Knowing she'd never be able to discuss their
loss openly with Paul, Maura took advantage of every
second that Pam spent listening to her.

The first few weeks dealt with slightly superficial
subjects but there was no rush to get Maura discussing
James. Pam was building the bond between them and
allowing Maura to decide when she felt ready to bring up
her loss. They talked first of Maura's childhood, how she
met Paul and the relationship they enjoyed. Every so
often, but usually too close to the end of the sessions,
Maura would mention something specifically about

James and the tears would spring to her eyes. Pam could tell that the time was approaching when Maura would follow through to wherever her talk of James took her. Maura, meanwhile, was enjoying getting to know Pam but perhaps more importantly she enjoyed speaking with another woman. She had pushed her few friends away and she didn't have a big network of support around her or any maternal guidance. Paul was a great husband but he never showed any empathy towards Maura in spite of their story. He dealt with loss by working harder, fighting his emotions and basically ignoring them. Maura on the other hand needed to talk. Needed to feel, needed to grieve openly for James.

Maura never asked Pam, or said anything at all to her, about what she had noticed after their first one-to-one session. She never had to say anything to be aware of Pam's understanding but respected her more for it. She could easily have just said out loud about her lost child and attempted to force the bond. Instead she left Maura to talk about herself during their sessions and Maura felt grateful to her for that.

Any time Maura began to speak of James, she felt overwhelmed by her emotions. But she could sense Pam willing her on and supporting her through. Pam could validate her every thought, emotion and belief. Paul would never return to the counselling road but this was ok with Maura as she was realising everybody needs to grieve in their own way.

Therefore what happened on the 12th session wasn't completely unexpected. Maura took control of the hour from the very beginning. Pam had entered the room where Maura was already sitting and asked her how she was feeling. That was all the invitation Maura needed to begin.

"I was about to say 'Ah yeah, I'm grand and how are you?' but that would've been a lie and I'd never be ready to begin this conversation. The truth is I'm miles away from ok. I'm completely devastated and heartbroken. My little boy was taken from me and I don't know how to deal with it. My husband is a great man but he doesn't know how to deal with James' death either. We just spend our days, weeks really, existing side by side. We've both lost our little boy but in spite of that shared grief, we're drifting further and further apart. I need to grieve, I need to feel loved and I need to be able to smile again. I certainly don't want to forget my James, I've lost him but I can't afford to lose myself and my husband over the same incident. I need your help Pam and I need to start living again."

12.

Paul arrived home late, as he always did, that evening. From the very beginning Maura knew that Paul enjoyed his pints and the atmosphere of being in the pub. He never watched sport and he had never had a crew of drinking buddies that he sat with. But Maura knew he was at his most comfortable on a high stool at the bar, with a pint in front of him; a newspaper to read or someone to talk to were always optional extras. He had the ability to sit and stare without talking and think through what was happening in his life. He relished the opportunities to take stock of his life and assess his position in the world. Since James passed away and he turned his back on the Church, his time in the pub was his way of coping and surviving.

He rarely left before closing time, more and more this had been in the hope that Maura had gone off to bed long before, having given up hope of him taking an early night. They'd hardly spoken at all in the last few months, never mind finding a way to talk about James. They hadn't touched each other in weeks. How could they when all they could see when looking at each other were shadows of their boy.

As Paul walked up their street he was surprised to see the light on in the sitting room. He was surprised but presumed Maura despite her normal conscientiousness had forgotten to switch it off. So when he opened the hall door and heard the television on and then saw Maura's shadow cast on the floor, shock rather than surprise was the emotion Paul felt.

"Wakey, wakey Maura! You've fallen asleep in front of the television for jaysus sake; I think it's time for bed!" Paul found a jauntiness in his voice and actions that wouldn't last. It was probably the couple of pints that gave him the confidence to have a laugh but he was very quickly set right about his actions.

Maura sat on the couch with her legs tucked underneath her. She looked almost foetal but she was definitely looking broken, vulnerable and terribly upset. Her cheeks were red and tear-stained. By the look of her Paul presumed she had been crying for a long time.

"Jaysus Maura love, what is it? As if I don't know what it is but is there something new or different that has upset you?"

"No Paul it's nothing new just the same thing, 'just' the death of our little boy." Maura wanted to come across as angry, as if Paul was trivialising their loss, instead in her timid voice she came across defeated and lost.

"Jaysus love of course I don't mean that James dying was something small or trivial" Paul responded, picking up on the subtlety of Maura's language despite the gallon of porter inside him. "I meant had anything particularly upset you today? I thought you were doing really well and being strong. I haven't wanted to ask you out straight in case I upset you more but is this a regular thing? Do you often cry when you are here alone?"

Paul had been standing since he entered the living room and now moved to sit on the couch beside Maura. He wanted to put his arm around her and comfort her but she was firm in her refusal to let that happen.

"Don't you fucking dare sit down beside me and try to solve this with a quick hug and some comforting words.

That won't work now, not a hope." Wordlessly Paul let his backside find the armchair. He didn't want to upset Maura anymore.

"It's 9 months since James died and we haven't had a proper conversation in the meantime. We sleep in the same house but we're not living together. I've lost my son but if I lost you as well, I wouldn't be able to go on. You said to me right back at the beginning that we'd have to get through it together but we've done nothing together. Well we did try one thing together but we know how that worked out for us…."

"Well yer one was a fucking eejit and I think we had a lucky escape with that one."

"She did have a bad day when we met her but it shouldn't have been a reason to rule out counselling in totality. In fact I know that is the case. There's something I've been keeping from you but it's time I brought you in on it. You're probably going to be angry and upset with me but please let me finish and then we can discuss it."

Maura set about telling Paul all about the counselling sessions she'd been having in an as matter of fact tone as she could muster. She told him how it had started with a phone call after their original couples' session. She quietly, but firmly, stopped Paul when he tried to point out how awful that first session had been.

Maura explained how she had gotten a sense of Pam's tragedy when she turned up to her rooms after arriving in Kilcastle. She told Paul about the bond she had felt with Pam and believed that Pam understood her as a fellow mother and that was why she had continued with the sessions.

"I know you were turned off by that first session Paul, which is understandable, but something about how honest her words seemed over the phone encouraged me. I knew your mind was made up Paul but I had to go through with this for myself. I spent lots of time just sitting with Pam and passing the time but tonight I took control. I started the session by telling the truth. I told her just what I've told you and even now I find it easier to talk about than it was earlier. It's time for us to look forward Paul. If you're not going to do the counselling, I don't mind, but it's going to help me and I'll be continuing."

In the years that would follow, Maura would remind Paul of how much his response at this point would continue to mean to her. She had expected him to be angry and resentful of her having lied to him. She had prepared herself to have to convince him about the benefit of the sessions. Instead he reacted in a calm, measured way, reminiscent of the man she had first known. He merely sat forward a little and began;

"I know you might have expected me to explode but I'm glad you told me to stay quiet because I had to take it all in. In some ways I think you're mad love to give yer one money for talking and making you cry in her sessions, BUT it's obviously having some benefit for you so what I think isn't important. We have to make this up as we go along. Who knows what's right and what's wrong? So whether it's me going down the pub or you going for a session of a different kind, we'll get there. This can't be allowed to come between us and it won't."

"How can you be so sure Paul? I mean we don't talk, we haven't had sex since, you know, God I'd love you to just hold me." Paul motioned towards her but was stopped in his tracks by Maura's wagging finger and cheeky smile, "and not just when you've had a few pints! Just give me a hug, show me you're here with me now and again."

Considering the distance that had grown between Paul and Maura in the years since that conversation, it was hard to believe how naïve they had been about what the future held in store for them. They eventually got a sex life back between them, if sex on their birthdays' and their anniversary qualified as a sex life. Paul had continued his grieving and growth in the pub. Maura meanwhile had sought out the local counselling services to continue her own journey. In all those years Paul never asked how Maura's sessions went and she never asked him about his nights in the pub. Two people living together, having two more kids together but all the while living very different lives.

13.

"This will never, ever fucking happen again." Paul slurred. "I'm not going to hide us away on any day of celebration again. All the pointing and whispering we had this morning and the false pity and everything else that goes with it. It won't happen ever again, I promise you." It was there and then the Forsyth's made one of the biggest decisions of their lives. Lying sprawled on the couch, half-drunk and with the Queen of England temporarily visiting their front room.

"You know what Paul? I think you may be right. I've tried to move on, I've tried to carry on and I've tried talking about it but the cycle just continues. We'll never forget our James but I hate that no one in this town will ever let us forget. I know they're only doing what they think they should but......"

"You're spot on Maura, I would give anything for someone to just ask me about the weather or better still ignore me completely like they used to."

"I'd love to go in and buy the milk and be treated like every customer. If that Walsh teenager that works in his Da's newsagents puts on his best empathetic face, tilts his head and asks me how I really am again I'll scream."

"That tilty head thing pisses me off too! I mean it's grand that you didn't know me before James died, just don't start pretending you care about me now."

"Do you know something else Paul? I think this might be the first time in months that we've actually spoken to each other about.... Well about anything really. We've been feeling and thinking the same things and yet we haven't been talking to each other, why is that?"

"I thought the hippie, love the world, chatting sessions you were doing were helping you so I just left you at it. I didn't want to burst your bubble if you fully believed in it."

"For a long time it was a good idea for me but the last while I haven't enjoyed it or gotten anything form it."

"Jaysus Maura! It's only taken us bottles of wine, crates of beer and feckin' Christmas to talk to each other properly. So you're not happy in the group, I'm not happy not being ignored in the pub and neither of us like the way the locals point at us and speak about us behind their hands, does that cover it all?"

"Absolutely!" Maura replied enthusiastically, if a little drunkenly, raising her glass to toast with Paul their sad state of affairs.

"Jaysus it's fucking awful so it is. Why don't we move?"

"Yeah let's go Paul, I'm right behind you. We'll live off the land and make our own clothes. We could even find a private island somewhere!"

"I'm being serious Maura, not to all that hippie shite but we can move to another town. A new village where no one knows us, nobody knows what we've been through and I can tell everyone that I'm just a lucky bastard married to an amazing wife!"

"You're actually been serious aren't you Paul? Even with a clatter of cans inside you!"

"That's because I do mean it Maura. Ignore the beer I've had and the red wine stains on your teeth and think about it. We move somewhere else and start again. WE will absolutely remember James and bring him with us but no one else will be able to remind us of because they won't know. It's not like we've any ties to this place, for jaysus sake it's Christmas day and we weren't invited to have dinner with anyone. There hasn't been a knock on the door to wish us a happy Christmas under the circumstances". Paul added the air quotes to the last three words for effect. "I've had it and I think you have too. We'll get through the holidays as best as we can and come the New Year we'll go looking for a new place to live."

"But can we really do that Paul? I mean where would we go?"

"That's it though, we can go anywhere really. Once Jimmy will write you a reference and I'm sure he'd help you find something new. I mean you've worked your ass off for him in that job and it's never enough. We can have a clean slate and start again, yeah?"

****

The opportunity for change and the freedom to start afresh came as a huge positive for both Paul and Maura. Maura had originally got a loan from Jimmy to start up her business but she was now ready to make a strike for it on her own. He had had the business experience and the contacts around him. He also had the money. Maura had the great ideas and the innovative plans but couldn't finance them herself. Jimmy (the) Fox was a bit of a local legend who Paul had met in the pub one evening. He never seemed to work and yet flashed cash all over the town. Maura had never taken to him but she had tolerated him as he put up the money for her cottage industry to grow.

Maura took great pleasure in being able to pick the moment she would drop the bombshell on Jimmy. She would be taking her skills and talents with her. A businessman with no culinary skills and no taste buds from years of smoking cigars, Jimmy would struggle to continue in the homemade bakery field after Maura left. She had spent two years watching and learning from Jimmy about running a business. Sometimes she learned what she should do and at other times, what she shouldn't. So when she sat in front of the Kilcastle Credit Union Board she was well prepared for any and all of their questions.

"I've got say Mrs. Forsyth," the Chairman commented, "your business plan is mighty impressive. The documents and the figures make sense but your passion and enthusiasm is also obvious. I think we'd be delighted to help you get started with a new business loan."

Maura skipped out of the meeting; excited at the prospect of baking her products to sell and not just that but the branding would have her name and hers alone on it. She was so wrapped up in the plans she almost made it past the coffee shop but she'd earned a little treat for herself. Plus now that she had the business plan approved, it would do no harm to check out the competition before she decided who to approach about stocking her goods.

After a lengthy discussion about the town's tastes, the benefits of fully home-made rather than processed and the interest in tea-rooms similar to those in the UK to indulge, Maura sat down with a pot of tea and a slice of baked cheesecake. It had taken little effort on her part to get the employee to divulge lots of valuable information to this innocent looking stranger.

As she sat nibbling at the cheesecake and sipping tea, Maura thought of James and smiled to herself, 'I know it's been tough but I really know you're there helping me out darling. You gave me the confidence to go in there and get my loan today. I know with your help I'll make this a success. Not to mention that this cheesecake can't compete with mine. It's too flaky, dry and bland. I need to get on with the conversion and start producing.'

Maura sat for a long time, cradling her tea in her hands, the smile never waning for a second. Nearly a year had passed since James' death and she continued to grieve for him every day. Generally this happened first thing in the morning when his absence was most pronounced. This however was the first time she'd come anywhere close to feeling content since the previous June. Paul and herself were settling into their new home. They'd introduced themselves to the neighbours as newlyweds who'd just moved into the area. Now with her business about to take off, Maura was praying that some form of normality would return to their lives.

Maura eventually rose to leave the coffee shop and waved a cheery goodbye to the waitress in the kitchen. Secretly she vowed to make sure her cakes would be sold there by Christmas. She pulled on her hat on what was an unseasonably cold morning and looked up at the clear sky above. 'You took great care of me today James, I hope you had enough time to look after your Dad too with his interview. You know as well as I do how much he needs that job, even if it is just portering in the nursing home. I better get home and see how he did.'

****

To call it an interview would be stretching the truth. Four questions, including 'when can you start?' hardly constituted a grilling. But Paul wasn't bothered at all. He needed to get out of the house, needed a job, any job. Maura was planning on moving forward with the home baking plan and he needed to do something himself. The first steps in their plan had all worked very well. They agreed an end date for their lease and began looking at where they might set up home. Where they were leaving was too rural so they knew they wanted a busy town but they definitely didn't want to move to a city, just close to one. Kilcastle ticked the most boxes and it had enough life and activity to keep them busy but they felt it was just big enough that they could feel anonymous too if they wanted. Nobody came to wish them well. There was little fanfare to their departure. If ever they wanted confirmation that they were doing the right thing then this was it. There was nothing tying them to Louth and no one begging them to stay. All the residents of the town knew them, at least to see, and they knew about the year they'd endured. Yet not one person stopped as they packed up to ask them what was happening. It was as if the locals were happy they wouldn't have to feel guilty for being happy any longer and were happy to see them go.
A new start and a clean slate was the best thing that could happen to them. As they unpacked their car

outside their new home in Kilcastle, the neighbours on both sides came out to introduce themselves. Paul and Maura said hello and enjoyed taking a break to have a chat. They described themselves as newlyweds setting up home and looking forward to their future together. And what was even better for them was that their new neighbours just accepted that as anybody would. There were no more questions about the past or their traumas. As Maura and Paul unpacked the last of the boxes and closed the door for their first night in their new home, Paul went to the kitchen to open a cold beer and pour Maura a glass of red wine. He walked into the sitting room with a massive grin on his face but he immediately saw that Maura was crying ever so slightly on the couch. "Are you alright love? I'm tired myself after a long day or did you get some dust from the boxes in your eye?"

"No it's nothing like that Paul, I'm just a little upset tonight. I know we're doing this for all the right reasons but did you notice how easy it was to lie to the neighbours? That can't be a good thing can it?"

"Probably not but it's not like WE are forgetting about James. We'll keep him alive in our heads but we've a chance at starting afresh here and our neighbours don't really care what happened before we arrived next door. Just imagine tomorrow morning walking down the street without whispering behind our back or anyone smiling falsely at us, no this is definitely the right decision for us."

"Yeah you're probably right, I'm just a little sad tonight but I'll be fine. Any chance we've a bottle of white wine outside? I was hoping one of the bottles we were given was white, a new start and a new drink and all that."

"I'll have a look, I think there might be but I can tell you for nothing I won't be moving off the stout. Wasn't it a bit of a rush being newlyweds again?" he called making his way to the kitchen. Maura pretended she didn't hear because it hadn't felt good. They weren't newly married and she didn't want to dismiss the previous five years together. Paul returned with her white wine and sat on the armchair, miles away and nothing like newlyweds Maura thought.

Paul thought about their move as he waited for his pint to settle in The Local. He could think of no better way to celebrate his new job. 'It might only be a night portering gig in the local nursing home but jaysus it's going to be a great way to stay out of the house and have less free time to think about James.'

Five pints later, Paul eventually decided it might be time to go home, time to share the good news with Maura. 'Ah bollix, Maura' he thought 'she was down the Credit Union today looking for a loan. 'Jaysus I hope she got it' he thought as he stumbled out the door of the pub. Yeah he could've gone straight home after his interview but in fairness he had to celebrate his good news. And raise a toast to his son for getting him the job. 'Thanks for minding me son.'

14.

Just three sessions into their new relationship Maura knew she could trust Pamela completely. Counselling and talk therapy were vital to her and Suzy had just been too raw and too naïve to bring her past a certain point in her journey. After leaving Ardee for Kilcastle, Maura had chanced a visit to see Pamela. What started that day as a patient/counsellor relationship had blossomed and grown into a mutually beneficial friendship over the intervening 23 years.

Very quickly it became obvious to Maura that Pam brought new ideas and fresh angles to many of the thoughts and processes she took for granted. The influence of the Church and its' role within the community was massive and to the forefront of life in Ireland in the early nineties. Even the counsellors who were agnostic and independent of the Church weren't always correct in that presumption. The Parish Priest would often refer parishioners to the counsellor while also offering the parish hall or community centre as a location to meet people.

Maura herself had found Pam through the Church. On arriving in Kilcastle she had introduced herself to Father Murphy after Mass and asked about the local groups and services that met up regularly. She didn't feel like asking out straight about bereavement groups and so listened just as intently as the priest ran through the range of services from bridge to adapted exercise.

But when Maura walked into Pam's own rooms, located in her garden and completely separate to any religious organisation, she felt happy at that prospect of having an independent view. Pam assured her that different services from different sources are required to ensure people received the most suitable support. Despite the separation Maura continued to ask questions about her own faith and her participation in church activities almost on a weekly basis. Rather than turn her off religion, as it had done for Paul, Maura found herself deeper and deeper into the subconscious of her thoughts and beliefs and questioning every aspect of her life.

Pam retired from counselling in 2005, if retiring is ever really possible. The old cornerstones of active listening, using silence to draw people out and open questions however were so habitual that she had difficulty at times being a friend rather than a counsellor to Maura. They had whiled away many hours talking this through. And because Pam had been such a fantastic mentor to Maura throughout her training, they sometimes slipped into the student/teacher relationship too.

This was in spite of their determined efforts to leave their jobs outside their relationship. Once the mind is used to questioning itself and life's conundrums however, it's a difficult switch to turn off. Which is why ten years after stopping seeing patients, Pam found she was asking Maura all about her latest bereavement session in the parish hall. "Go on Maura, tell me about it, I know you want to and I'm here to listen."

Maura chuckled at the language Pam used, so reminiscent of her own introductions but then she got back to the subject at hand. "We've had a very settled group and turnout over the last 6-9 months. Generally it's been the same people trying to help each other through their grief together. On Monday night a young fella came into the room like a whirlwind of energy breaking the settled calm of our group. He was fidgety and nervous and almost hyperactive. I'd imagine his doctor had given him a little something to boost him but maybe got the dosage wrong.

Anyway as the session began he sat himself down but he was constantly rubbing his hands together, scratching at invisible stubble and shifting in his seat. He seemed so uncomfortable but I respected him for getting there at all. All the others in the group began to pick up on the fact he was taking over the group and drawing attention to himself, despite not saying a word.

So when a gap arrived in the conversation I took the opportunity to see if he wanted to introduce himself and say why he found himself there that night. Well, Pam, you wouldn't believe what happened next. He went off on a diatribe about this, that and everything else. It's a long time since I've seen someone so angry and bitter. He was angry at the world, angry at his fate, angry at everything that had led him to entering the session on Monday night.

There was frustration there too and it was a big mix of emotions. But despite the bluster and bravado he tried to exude he was no different to anyone else that comes in to see me. They're all somewhere on the road through grief and it doesn't matter how long they've been on the road they can be found anywhere. Sure I'm the same myself, as you well know Pam, even after 25 years I'm still dealing with James's death."

"It's not that long ago now is it? Jesus Christ I can still remember the first time I saw you inch your way into my rooms. I think you cried your way through our early sessions before you really started talking. You just needed to start somewhere and you did."

"Absolutely Pam, it's a long way from those one-on-one sessions to leading the bereavement group but nothing really changes though does it? Grief still has its' stages and signposts to negotiate and though he was angry and frustrated we'll be able to move him forward at some point when he is ready. He was railing and fighting against the world but beneath it all I recognised the sadness and frustration behind his words.

But then something beautiful happened. The group showed its' maturity and strength. They let him rant and vent his feelings and then without talking directly to him they began to show that the anger and frustration were universal, just as much as the sadness and the 'why me' questions. He quieted down and listened intently to the conversation going on around him. Slowly but surely his anger and bitterness receded and the full extent of his loss began to hit home.

A frightened, broken and emotionally tormented young man lurked behind the façade. He couldn't cope with his loss and had chosen to minimize and deny it in the hope that he might wake from this awful nightmare. But as he listened to the reality of coping with the loss of a child he heard that no matter when it happens, it is real, it hurts and it takes great courage and strength to try and find a way to deal with the sadness.

The full magnitude of his loss began to hit him and he sat, arms-folded around his stomach, crying silent tears for the loss of his little one. I wanted him to be relieved of some of the burden he was carrying. Just before we finished up for the evening I asked what had brought him to the group this Monday night. He just replied that he couldn't in front of her in case she saw it as weakness. He had to be strong to protect her from the sadness. One of the group asked who he was talking about. It turns out that not only had he lost a child when his wife miscarried but that they had also split up too and he was battling a double loss. He had blamed her but instantly berated himself for that. He felt guilty about the stress he had caused her too. He was angry that it happened at all and angry at the wedge it drove between them. And he was sad. Sad that his plans of the countryside idyll wouldn't come to pass and sad that he and his childhood sweetheart hadn't been able to paper over the cracks in their relationship the miscarriage magnified.

It was a tough session for him but I think it was vital too as it allowed the process of mourning, which I don't think he had done at all, to begin. He even thanked me through his tear-stained eyes as we finished up the session. We left the parish hall together and I think I can help this young lad out, I mean he's only about 25/26. As I reached the end of the path to turn for home, I spotted Paul under a tree waiting to walk me home. He never does that but I was glad of it after the session I'd just had. He'd had a tough 24 hours himself after Patricia's funeral and the rest so he didn't fancy The Local.

He asked about the young fella I'd left with and said he'd looked very upset. I just told him it was his first session and that he wouldn't be at the meeting if he wasn't upset. He seemed to accept that but I think he wanted to ask more questions about the lad. As much as he dismisses my work as rubbish, something about the young lad piqued his interest. Or maybe it was just that he was close to the age James would be, I don't know really."

"I'm afraid we'll have to leave it there for this week." Pam finally spoke up. They both laughed at the long speech Maura had broken in to and how this chat had definitely been more of a counselling session than two friends catching up. "Don't worry about paying me this week but if this happens again I'm charging you the full rate." With that the two friends laughed together and sipped on their tea; simultaneously, of course.

15.

"Fucking hell! Have you not been killed off yet?"
Paul would have responded but the short arm jab he'd
received to the kidneys temporarily knocked the wind
out of his sails. Eventually he got his coat off and turned
to face his attacker. "You keep hitting me like that every
Thursday evening George and you'll get closest to
finishing me."
Paul was giving away the best part of 20 years to retired
detective George Dalton but his reputation as having
hands as big as shovels and as hard as nails was well
earned. He doled out a so-called friendly jab into Paul
every Thursday evening and going by the way it took his
breath away, retirement hadn't softened him at all.
He'd often hang around after the Thursday afternoon
sessions had finished to complain, good-naturedly, about
having to pay full price for his last few pints. George
said he only stayed on if he was in good form or if he
needed a bit of quiet before heading home. But Paul
struggled to remember any Thursday evening when he
hadn't been there.
"Are you putting in for overtime again tonight then
yeah?" Paul asked as usual.
"Absolutely Paul, but I'm working an undercover sting
so if anyone asks you, you've no idea who I am right?"
George replied as usual.
"No bother at all George, I'll keep it zipped!" Nothing if
not traditional older men, Paul and George acted out this
little scene, almost word for word, each week. If there
did happen to be a Thursday when George went home

before Paul arrived, he'd probably miss him. Though they'd never sat in each other's company for a pint, they enjoyed repeating the old lines.

"Was it another good session today George?"

"Yeah we'd a few pints, plenty of singing and a bit of cabaret added in today. Gerry and Ger forgot their hearing aids so they were sat at the bar screaming at each other from a yard away! Willie was halfway through the Auld Triangle when they interrupted him with Gerry asking what she was cooking for dinner, and Ger trying to tell him they were having chops!"

"Jaysus after an afternoon like that, you'll be needing a few quiet pints now I'm sure? Do they taste any better after the others leave and you're left paying full price? Tell you what, just for a change I'll leave alone to read the paper, fair enough?"

"Only if you're sure now Paul?" Neither man would've known what to talk to each other about if they had actually sat together. Instead, they chuckled to themselves and George finished his journey from the toilets back to his seat on the other side of the front door to Brian O'Neill's.

Paul watched him back to his seat, he wasn't a young man after all, and was about to fix his gaze back on Andy to put on a pint, when he saw a head bob along the window at the front of The Local. A vague sense of recognition swept over him. Where did he know that head from? Was it a regular in the pub or did he just recognise the appearance of one the residents he passed wordlessly on the street day after day. He was mid-toast to James and nearly on the first sip of the day when he heard a voice he thought was aimed at him.

"Excuse me? I'm sorry to disturb you but I just wanted to apologise for the messing last Sunday afternoon." Padraig was the owner of the floating head outside the window who had now disturbed him.

"Listen all I want to do is have a few quiet pints on my own, so just forget about it and move on."

"That's all I want myself too, but I just wanted to be sure sir. I've been a bit all over the place recently and I was so frustrated I was spoiling for a fight. I didn't know anything about the little one dying 'cos I've been so self-involved, the death of a child is always terrible and I shouldn't have been rowing with you over that but I just wanted to vent."

"Fair enough son, I didn't come out of it too well either, I just couldn't figure out why you'd be so angry about the pub being closed for any child's funeral."

"I know, I know, in fact I probably know better than most sir but I'll leave you be and at least now we can drink in the same pub. Good luck." Padraig turned to move down the counter to sit, while Paul turned to face him properly for the first time since he walked into the bar.

"Just before you move there son" Paul spoke up and Padraig turned once more. "There's no need to be calling me sir ok? I'm old but I'm not someone you should be respecting too much." As he spoke Paul felt a wave of recognition sweep over him while he looked at Padraig. "It was you wasn't it? It was you I saw coming out of the Bereavement Counselling group on Monday night?"

"What are you on about mate? That wasn't me at all, why would I be at a session like that?"

"Well I couldn't know that son but I did see you coming out with my wife afterwards. That lad was pretty upset and now I look at you properly, if it's not you it was your twin. I'm not in to all that talking therapy shite but I've no problem having a pint so maybe you'd join me for one?"

"What the fuck are you on about? You following me or something? It wasn't me anyway, whoever you saw." Padraig was trying to bluff his way out of an awkward situation but the indignation seemed feigned and his quivering lip gave the whole game away.

"It's up to yourself son but if you don't want to drink on your own, there's a seat free for you there beside me." Paul tapped the stool beside him showing exactly what was on offer.

"What are the chances you saw me? Where were you? I thought that'd be a private thing for me to do and….."

"My wife is the group facilitator and I went to meet her after the session on Monday. She never normally leaves alone so no one knows which evening class people are leaving from. But I saw her leaving with a very upset young lad and then when I looked at you properly tonight I recognised you."

"Maura's your wife? For fuck's sake this town is too fucking small! Did she go home and spill the beans about all my difficulties and loss?"

"So it was you then? First things first, Maura doesn't say a word about anyone she meets, not a word. I don't believe in any of the talking stuff but she does and she loves helping people out. If it was me I'd much rather be here having a pint instead. Sit down there son and stop making me nervous standing over me. If you don't want to talk about your shite, grand, but let me get you a pint anyhow."

Padraig retrieved his jacket and sat up next to Paul as they introduced themselves properly and Paul ordered a couple of pints. "I don't talk to anyone in this pub really Padraig but maybe Patricia's death has me a bit shook too, so if you want to talk, work away."

"You've got to admit it's a bit fucking mad Paul, I'm only after moving in and I don't know many people but the two I've spoken to most are fucking married?!"

"It's definitely a small town alright but you've been mighty unlucky son. What made you pick our town to pitch your tent?"

"I'd my life all laid out before me, living with my wife further up north. When we ran into the first difficulties our relationship had ever really had, I didn't cope very well at all. We'd planned for years to move to where we did in the countryside and when we'd have all our kids."

"Did something happen to your wife Padraig? Is that why you were at the bereavement session?"

"No, no it was nothing like that, well not completely. She had a miscarriage about 2 months ago now and it's the reason I moved here and the reason I was at the session. Everyone told me she did nothing wrong but I blame her, blamed her, and our relationship really suffered. I didn't react well and we started to row a lot, every little quirk and mannerism irritated the other and became massive issues and it was the end of our relationship, our marriage."

"Bloody hell, you've lost a lot in a short period of time son. But is the bereavement group the right place for you to be working through a miscarriage? I mean do the others in the group see it as a real loss? Would Brian O'Neill see his loss as the same as yours?"

"Almost definitely not I'm sure but I needed to start somewhere and thankfully your wife, and the group, let me talk and share on Monday without questioning it. I'm grieving for the life we planned which will never happen now. I'm grieving for the end of my marriage to Sinead, the only woman I've ever loved. I'm grieving for a lot of things."

"Yeah that's fair enough but could you not have just tried again for a baby? This time next year you both could have been parents?"

"Yeah maybe so Paul but it turns out putting it as bluntly as that a week after the miscarriage doesn't go down too well! I can't believe I'm just telling you all this, you're as good a listener as your wife is."

"Steady on now, don't be going soft on me now, I'm just here for the pints! But something did hit me when I saw, who turned out to be, you so upset on Monday. Loss at any age is tough but especially if it's of someone young or if you're young yourself. In saying that though, if you want to talk feelings and emotions go talk to my wife on a Monday but if you're happy enough to sit in silence and talk bollocks every so often I pretty much live on this stool."

"Cheers Paul, I appreciate the blunt honesty! I don't think they'll be welcoming me back on Monday evenings but I might see your wife on a one-to-one basis and it'll be nice to know someone in here when I come in for a beer."

"Blunt honesty is the only way to go. Deal with the issue and move on is what I've always done but maybe there's more than one way to do things. Now are you drinking that pint or just picking it up now and again?" Paul ordered two more pints off Andy and sat back as Padraig tried to put a hole in the pint in front of him before the next one arrived. 'This lad appears while I'm talking to you James and he's about the same age you'd be now, is God a man for the practical jokes or is this just a massive coincidence? Actually son, it doesn't matter either way, I'll talk to you soon.'

16.

He was sprinting now. Not with his legs so much as in his mind. A thousand thoughts a second were sprinting through his brain and despite walking as fast as he could, he couldn't move as quickly as he wanted. He felt claustrophobic and he felt nauseous. There was no way they could know. They couldn't have known his history. But..

But when they spoke Padraig felt like he was being chastised from the pulpit. The only man in the congregation. A bold schoolboy forced to make his first confession. Like a schoolboy his cheeks reddened as the conversation carried on.

Even the dark interior of The Local didn't make him feel any better. He felt the others could see his shame as clear as day. Paul and himself were having a great chat and even Charlie was joining in but something in the way they were talking had got in on Padraig. He had felt they were talking about him personally. Talking about his life, talking about his emotions. 'How do they know what I've gone through in the last year? How do they know the range of emotions I've gone through this past year? Jesus they could have spoken to the parish priest back in Cavan they know so much, or at least seem to know! But Fr. Case lives by the confidentiality of the confession box.'

Eighteen months ago his future had been laid out in front of him. Sinead and himself had moved to the rolling countryside of County Cavan. They were in search of the idyll that so many people like to imagine. They had no kids yet but their lives were in front of them and buying a big house on its' own land was the first step on that road.

For the first six weeks in their new home, Sinead and Padraig acted like the newlyweds they were. They christened every room in their house, twice over, and enjoyed the freedom and freshness that living in the country afforded them. They enjoyed every second of their sex life. If this was practising for the day they'd conceive, then they were happy to spend the time perfecting their technique and learning all about each other's bodies.

Padraig was happy to have found a woman with as high a sex drive as him. But there was always something nagging away at him in the back of his mind. Even on those perfect weekends when they barely left the bedroom to eat, he'd hoped desperately that that would be the weekend. That at some point in the following few weeks he'd get the call he longed for.

All Padraig had wanted to be for as long as he could remember was to be a father. He wished he could take his child to kick a football, jump in a lake or go camping with. The idea of passing on information and being the source of guidance and advice was what he lived for. He loved Sinead dearly but he knew that love would be dwarfed by his love for HIS child. They tried and tried to conceive for many months. They tried diets and fads, drinks and supplements. They did everything in their power but slowly but surely they both began to wonder if there may be a reason why it wouldn't happen for them. They talked around the subject but eventually after one of those long, slow Sunday mornings spent making love

Padraig decided he wanted to broach the subject head on. He held Sinead close, gently kissed the nape of her neck and began;
"I know we don't really want to have this conversation but I think we have to at this stage." He put his left arm around her naked body just below her breasts and felt her heart rate increase. His right was trapped under her body, a familiar spot for all men, but he gently stoked her face with his fingertips. "I don't want to upset you love but we have to think about getting checked to see if there is a particular reason we haven't gotten pregnant"
"I know, I know" was about all Sinead could whisper in reply. They held each other tight not wanting to let go of their feelings of guilt and fear about upsetting each other. Sinead felt guilty because she knew how much Padraig wanted children and she so desperately wanted to provide him with them. It was her job as his wife to do this, or so she thought. She had often wondered if it was her fault they hadn't been successful in conceiving. Padraig meanwhile felt guilty for the pressure he had put on Sinead to get pregnant. It wasn't his fault he wanted children, in fact he thought that Sinead would prefer that. But he felt guilty for talking about it so much and so loudly in the early days of their relationship. Instead of relaxing and letting whatever would be, be, he had put intense pressure on both of them to reproduce. As a result what had once been expressions of their love had become monthly exams of virility. That brought its' own stresses and anxieties which made conception difficult and led to a vicious cycle of despair.
Making love became a function, a chore with no sense of pleasure or excitement. A good sex life was now defined

as resulting in pregnancy, not pleasuring each other in new ways and enjoying the vitality of youth. They stopped looking forward to sex with any sense of anticipation and as a result this conversation had become inevitable. No matter how difficult a conversation it would be.

"This has been going on too long for something not to be wrong hasn't it?" After a long silence Sinead finally broke the ice. They were both so timid and afraid of saying something to upset or offend the other that every single word they spoke was considered and delivered in as neutral a tone of voice as possible.

"Yeah you're probably right love, I don't know for sure but it's probably time to consider that possibility."

"I love you with all my heart but I feel so bad for not giving you a child of your own."

"A child of OUR own Sin, I want us to be parents. And there's no knowing why we can't conceive. It could be you, it could be me or it could just be a combination of the two of us. That's IF we even have a problem."

They were clawing at slippery ground trying desperately to remove any blame or the possibility of blame from the conversation. Padraig wrapped her tightly in his arms as she spoke. Showing her better than he could ever express in words how much he loved and cared for his wife.

"There's probably only one thing to do so love. We'll make an appointment to see Dr McCall. I've no idea how to go about checking us out but he'll know the process I'm sure and be able to point us in the right direction."

"Yeah he'll point us out the door and head straight to the pub to tell everyone about our troubles. He's as old as my parents, older in fact, and knows nothing about

Doctor/Patient confidentiality. He's been filling Mammy in on all the ladies in her bridge team every time she sees him. No if we've to go all the way into a hospital or somewhere we will. I don't want anyone knowing our business. Or even worse, they'd be looking me up and down as I walk down the town wondering if I'm FINALLY pregnant!"

"Okay, okay that probably makes sense. I'd never even considered that possibility but now you say it I have heard him showing a few tales down in O'Sheas after a few pints."

"Exactly and imagine if any of our friends or my parents overheard that conversation. All Mam asks me know is 'well? Are you?' It just heaps the pressure on and imagine she knew we were going to get some tests done, she'd be all over us like a rash and getting in the way. I couldn't stand her or anyone else knowing our business."

"Yeah that's fair enough Sin; we've already put enough pressure on ourselves without doing anything to add to it. I'll take a look online and make an appointment for us to someone who knows the score."

They lay in silence for a few minutes before Sinead began to giggle a little and Padraig could feel her body shaking. "What are you giggling at?" he asked, delighted to hear his wife's throaty giggle again.

"You know you'll probably have to, you know, go in a cup?"

"Don't be worrying about me" he whispered back "I had plenty of practice with that before we got together love!"

"Yeah you did I'm sure! Just think you'll have had sex with as many cups as women after that. Pity I can't get any feedback from the cup about your 'moves' and if you are actually any good or is it that I just don't know any better!"

"What moves like this?" Padraig asked as he pushed himself up using his hands to pin hers' above her head "We may as well keep practicing in the meantime eh?" Sinead felt him kiss her neck and knowing it wasn't really a question, gave her assent with just a small moan of pleasure.

17.

The phone call confirming the news he had been waiting on for months finally arrived. Padraig sat behind his desk, grinning from ear to ear. Padraig had recognised Sinead's number on his mobile and remembering the stupid row they had had that morning, he presumed she was ringing to apologise. He wasn't going to make it easy for her though so answered the phone with a curt "what?"

Sinead knew how petty a man he could be and so had expected something like that when she called. She knew all that pettiness and point scoring would melt away to inconsequentiality once she said her first three words. "I'm pregnant Podge!"

"You're kidding? That's unbelievable news, oh my God we've waited so long for this moment and finally we've been blessed with what we've always wanted. How many weeks are you? When's our due date?" Padraig had completely forgotten about that morning's row. He had never tried to mask his excitement at becoming a father so Sinead wasn't surprised by his somewhat over the top response.

"I'm only a couple of weeks late darling so you've got to keep this to yourself, I'm so excited too but we can't tell anyone else for a while yet, I mean it's very early days yet. It will be great but we should keep it to ourselves so we don't build up any false hopes for anyone. We're going to be parents and all the work we've done over the years to get the house will be worth it. I didn't want to tell you before I went to the Doctor because although I was late and feeling nauseated, I couldn't have dealt with thinking it and then finding out it was a false positive or something."

"But it's been fine love and this is going to be an amazing experience. How am I going to cope not telling me people, we've wanted kids for so long and now finally all those gossips asking why we haven't had kids yet can be put back in their box. When can we tell people? Are we supposed to wait about 12 weeks isn't it? I think I remember that from one of the books."

"Fucking hell, you read more of those books than I did and I'm the one going to be carrying the child! Just keep it under your hat for now, we'll tell everyone and our parents too after the 12 week scan."

"Can I not even tell them? I mean they'll be so happy we're finally starting our family."

"Will you stop saying finally Padraig? You're as bad as the rest of them. It hasn't been for the lack of trying I haven't got pregnant and that's probably another reason not to tell anyone too soon, okay?"

"I'm just excited babe but if you don't want me telling anyone I'll keep it quiet. It's all about you now, and the little one of course, whatever they need, they come first, no question at all."

They talked for another few minutes before Sinead hung up the phone but she was amazed that in a single phone call Padraig had managed to reduce her to the role of incubator and not the object of his love and the one he should be channelling his efforts in to. Padraig on the other hand was oblivious to his verbal slip. The smile stayed painted across his face all day. Finally his wife had got pregnant and finally he'd be the father he wanted to be. The major problem for him would be keeping the news quiet for another few weeks.

The first change to become noticeable in the McGrath's life was the increased phone calls. It felt like every five minutes and every time Sinead moved the phone would ring. She hadn't a second to herself; Padraig wanted an update on everything. From how many times she had thrown up that morning to how stressed she was and even to asking did she feel she was providing a 'safe, relaxed environment for their little gift.' If she wasn't already suffering through horrible morning sickness this line from his favourite baby book would've got her there.

"Morning babe, how are you feeling? You were asleep when I left this morning and I didn't want to wake you when you looked so peaceful. Is everything ok? Did you get in to work alright?"

"Didn't I answer the shop phone Padraig? So what would you think? I got up after you left, threw up for about a half hour and now I'm trying to get on and do a bit of work." The weariness shone through Sinead's words.

"Good, good, ok that's great. Are you getting enough breaks and staying off your feet before you go too long?"

"Of course I am Padraig, same as I've always done. For Christ's sake, Mary doesn't run a slave labour camp here. If I want to sit down behind the till for 5 minutes I can, exactly the same as I could have done 6 months ago. Plus I'm only four weeks gone, there's no need for me to be going around in bubble wrap!"

"Yeah but it's not just yourself to consider now though is it?"

"I suppose not Padraig, but the tiny fecking seahorse inside me now isn't exactly a 9lb baby about to be born is it? Listen I've got to go, Mary is just coming back in from the storeroom." Sinead replaced the receiver and took a breath before he had chance to reply. She composed herself and spotting a teenager looking at the scarves like a lost child, she went off to make a sale. Mary arrived back to the checkout with the box of reduction stickers for the weekend sale. "Was that another personal call Sinead?" Mary was asking but she knew the answer, and she made no effort to hide her irritation at the amount of times Sinead was getting distracted from her job by Padraig's calls. Sinead continued towards the lad probably looking for a present for his mother with her smile in place, but underneath she couldn't help but agree with Mary and her frustration directed at Paul.

****

"Good morning can I speak to Sinead please?" Mary had never met Padraig in person but knew instantly who she was speaking to. Three weeks of 5/6 calls a day had seen to that. Seeing nobody in the shop to overhear, Mary saw an opportunity.
"No you can't!" she snapped. "Your wife is gone to the toilet but I'm glad I got to pick up the phone to you today. I've never met you, only spoken to you on the phone a couple of times but this has got to stop. Sinead's got a job to do here, which she really enjoys but she can't get on with it if you keep ringing to speak to her

every five minutes. How do you even have the time to do that when you're at work yourself?"

"I just want to make sure she's doing ok and feeling good."

"There are some difficult times ahead for her alright but she's about 6 weeks pregnant not after major health scare."

"She's told you she's pregnant?" Padraig felt hurt that Sinead had told someone when he had been so guarded with the information.

"Well yeah she did tell me, but that came after I'd figured it out for myself genius. I saw my friend looking flushed every morning, I saw my friend using the bathroom more often and I saw my friends over-bearing, suffocating husband, begin to call my shop twenty times a day so I asked her and Sinead confirmed it to me. She didn't deliberately set out to tell me but we spend 9 hours a day together so it wasn't too hard to figure out what was happening. So just do us both a favour and stop calling every five minutes to check up on her, ok?"

Padraig was stunned but agreed to stop calling as often but insisted that he would still be calling. Women want men to care and feel involved in the pregnancy and now he was being told to back off a bit, how could he get in trouble for caring too much? But he now knew for certain, he'd be telling the lads when they went for their pint after work.

That evening Padraig found himself two and a half pints down and with a tongue that was loosening by the second. Dave sat across from him, forcing himself to sip at a pint. He definitely didn't want to be there with Padraig any more than the rest of the office but they had been in much quicker with their various excuses. So he found himself alone in the pub with the boss, a soldier left behind with the enemy.

Padraig had been giddy and full of energy around the office all afternoon. The type of shit that pissed off the whole staff, even more so than his demanding, gruff attitude. Dave had steeled himself for more chats about Padraig's 'perfect' wife, the family home which 'isn't just a house' on the outskirts of town and how the recession hadn't really touched their lifestyle.

Dave thought about this as he sipped his way through the one pint of cheap lager he'd be drinking tonight. He never went to the pub on a Tuesday and he knew that Ellie had precise plans for their funds for the rest of the week, the last week of the month thankfully. Dave was disgusted he was wasting some of his beer ration on a fucking Tuesday, with Padraig the Prick for company. He didn't think the €3 bargain beer could ever taste worse than normal but he was being proved wrong tonight.

18.

Padraig returned from the bar with a fresh pint and Dave found himself looking longingly at the fresh, appetising beer. Then he noticed that his boss, the ignorant prick, had a whiskey in his other hand to go along with his pint. 'And only one too? Fuck me. This tool could've bought me a pint of flavoured water no problem.' Dave thought to himself.

"It's brilliant to get out about on a Tuesday evening isn't it Dave? A few cheeky pints to kick-start the week, and what's more my missus will be home first so she'll get the dinner started, the same for you I'm sure Dave yeah?"

"Ah yeah, something like that alright. In fairness to Ellie she'll usually have something on for my dinner." Dave replied, neglecting to tell Padraig that Ellie would've been at home all day, trying to figure out how to make 3 slices of nearly stale bread, a tin of tomatoes and a tin of sardines into some sort of meal. She'd do it though, her resourcefulness never failed to impress Dave.

"I suppose you're wondering why I suggested a few pints this evening Dave?"

"Not really Padraig, I just presumed you'd had a big weekend and needed the cure." Dave couldn't have cared less about his boss's weekend or why they were having a pint but he really hoped he'd get to the point quickly so he could escape home.

"Well," Padraig began, enjoying the command of his stage but kind of wishing there was a bigger audience than just Dave. But he knew Dave looked up to him like a mentor so he'd appreciate being on the inside of the scoop. "You know the way myself and the beautiful Sinead got married and bought that big home outside of town when I got this job? Well the time has come to start filling up the bedrooms with our children." Padraig looked across at Dave but he didn't seem to be following so he explained further, "Sinead's pregnant! Isn't it great news? Now it's only early days so I can't be going around telling everybody but if Sinead can tell someone then I can too."

Dave declined the opportunity to remind Padraig that he hadn't been selected or singled out for some sort of honour; he'd merely been the slowest to come up with an excuse. Padraig was going on like they were best mates and he was party to some sort of awesome secret. Somehow he ignored those thoughts.

"Congratulations to you both! It's brilliant news for you and hopefully everything goes well for you both now. Dave raised his glass to salute Padraig's virulence and hoped he'd notice that Dave was doing so with a glass that was practically empty, while his own was still untouched, as was his whiskey. It didn't matter because he didn't notice it anyway.

Dave wanted to bolt for the door immediately but he was too polite for that. He couldn't give a fuck about Perfect Padraig or his life. He was struggling to manage to fend for himself and Ellie as it was. The idea of adding children in to that mix was terrifying for him and yet here was this dickhead rubbing his nose in it. And on a Tuesday too.

"It's great news Padraig and give my congratulations to Sinead too but I've got to hit the road and get home now."

"But I've just got fresh drinks in Dave; you wouldn't leave me to drink on my own now would you?" These were the words that came out of his mouth but Padraig was smiling and they both knew that he had to leave now. Padraig enjoyed an audience but it was clear to Dave he had served his purpose for the evening in listening to Padraig.

"Ah I'm sure you'll be fine Padraig, you'll enjoy them just as much without me and anyway you've one for each hand now!" Dave turned on his heel and didn't bother looking back. He couldn't resist having just a little dig but to maintain it was a joke tomorrow in the office he couldn't turn around to see if it had landed. Even still it felt good to say something to Padraig the Prick about his perfect life.

Dave's snipe at Padraig slipped under his radar. Padraig was quite comfortable in the buzz of his five pints, enjoying the evening as he had planned. Downing the whiskey in one, he made his way to the bar again. "Oi! Gimme a whiskey there will you?" Padraig was completely oblivious to the other customers sitting at the counter that he bumped in to or that the barman was busy serving someone else. He placed the tumbler on the counter unsteadily, the beer was hitting him alright but he was so happy he felt bulletproof. He was happy to ¯have told someone about his good news but he was delighted that Dave had had the good manners to piss off once he'd told him.

Eventually the barman made his way down to serve Padraig. He wanted to know who had been calling for him. He didn't want any of the regulars to think they could get away with mouthing off at him like that. "Sorry that was me boss, lost the run of myself but I'm just in good form, won't happen again, promise, will you throw a whiskey in there for me, make it a double." He paid for his drink and made for his table again. He didn't get that far.

He stumbled and spilled some of the precious nectar down a customer's back, kicked a leg of a table which sent a glass falling to the floor, then pulled his chair out too fast and rammed it into the customer behind him. With all the regulars now upset, Padraig didn't have much time left in the pub for tonight. The barman made a beeline for him and subtly coaxed him out of the pub. "Go on home you fuckin' eejit! You'd swear you were the first man to get his wife pregnant! Fuck it, if the kid's lucky it won't even be yours!"

Padraig left the pub behind, the laughter of the regulars echoing in his head all the way home. More than a little merry he crashed in through his front door and home to his newly with-child wife. "Where are you Sinead and we can have a ride to celebrate our great news? We could do it in the armchair like the good old days, what do you say?" As Padraig found the handle at the third attempt and barged into the living room, Sinead didn't need to say anything for him to know how that would go. There he found his wife, and parents-in-law, sipping tea from china cups. Not to mention his father-in-law, Noel, shifting uneasily on the armchair. "You didn't get my text about my parents coming over then I take it?" Sinead asked.

"Of course he didn't, or else he just ignored it, which would be true to form for the most self-centred man I've ever come across. Come on Elizabeth it's time for us to go."

"Wait, wait, please sit down, and don't leave on my account. I've had too much celebrating with the lads from the office and then I made things a hundred times worse with my crude comment. If I may I'd like to start again." With a flourish he left the room, opened the front door and closed it again, very gently. He never let go of the sitting room handle though in case he couldn't find it again. He took his phone from his pocket and studied it as he re-entered the living room.

"Elizabeth, Noel, thanks so much for coming over to celebrate with us. I'm only after seeing Jane's text there now; otherwise I'd have left the others in the pub hours ago. I've had one or two too many shandies so I'll make a pot of coffee. Would anyone else like one or just me?" Padraig was on full charm offensive and Sinead could see how he was such a good salesman.

Receiving no reply Padraig made for the kitchen, happy to have retrieved the situation with his in-laws, to some degree. As he pulled the door closed he heard Noel give him another going over but Sinead stood up for him in the best way possible.

"Fuck me, sorry Liz; he's some smarmy little git. I know you love him Sinead but there are times I'd love to floor him."

"I know he's a chancer and a smooth talker Dad but that's what got us the money for this place. Not forgetting that he's the father of this little bundle of joy. I mean you couldn't stay mad at the father of your first grandchild now could you?"

116

19.

'What does that bitch want now?' Padraig had seen the caller ID on his mobile and he didn't fancy answering. Mary never rang him. She certainly never rang him with good intentions. Sinead had worked with her for 2 and a bit years and the only time she rang was when she wanted to arrange a girlie night as a surprise for Sinead. Padraig hated those nights; usually they happened for Sinead's birthday, when he was exiled from his own house for the evening.

He had spent years saving to buy that house for himself, Sinead and their family, yet Mary would still insist he made himself scarce so the girls could chat. She had called Padraig a couple of times in the last few weeks, which was a massive increase. But these calls had angered Padraig even more than the annual birthday calls.

These times Mary was calling him to admonish him for having the cheek to call his wife at work. Who was she to be telling him that he couldn't call to check on his wife and the little person growing inside her, he thought. 'What's wrong with me ringing a couple of times a day for that? It's not as if I treat her badly, in fact it seems to be the other way around. Mary seems more pissed off that I care too much for Sinead.'

Just before his voicemail clicked in, Padraig saw Mary had disconnected the call and he felt a victorious emotion wash over him. Instantly the phone began ringing again, the loud chiming of his ringtone, strong and insistent. Mary was determined to give him her two cents worth.

"What is it this time?" he barked into the receiver, pleasantries and small talk an unnecessary addition to a conversation with Mary.

"Stop being so childish Padraig and listen to me…"

"Me being childish? You're the one going behind Sinead's back to tell me to stop calling. You're probably filling her head with all sorts of nonsense in there aren't you?"

"No I'm not you fucking gobshite, just shut up and listen for a change. I had to call you; I had to speak to you…"

"Yeah and I HAD to let your call go to voicemail but you wouldn't even let me do that would you?"

"Just listen will you for fucks sake? I had to get speaking to you straight away Padraig, a voicemail wouldn't cut it. It's Sinead, Padraig; I think she's in trouble with the baby…."

"What the fuck happened to her? Was she lifting boxes again or drinking coffee or something?" Padraig began to slowly pick up on the seriousness of Mary's call and a hundred questions ran around his head. "Okay, catch me up on what happened, no, where is she, no, how come you're on the phone not Sinead? Is she not able to talk?"

"This is a big shock for all of us Padraig and it's not sinking in yet. Just take a breath and I'll tell you what happened. She was tidying up a few bits in the changing rooms when it began. She's lost a lot of blood and she's really upset. She called me in and then she asked me to ring you and fill you in. I'm just locking the front door of the shop now, do you want me to see if she wants to talk to you or will you be able to get over to here?"

"I can't believe it, I can't believe it! This isn't supposed to be the way things go! Please go in to her Mary, I need to speak to my girl."

"Ok Padraig I'll go in to her now."

Padraig heard the pain and sadness of his wife flowing from her long before Mary got near her with the phone. He had never really seen or heard Sinead in pain before but he could tell from her frantic breathing and tears that she was as terrified as she was in pain. He tried shouting into the phone but Mary was walking with the mobile by her side and couldn't hear. By the time she handed the phone to Sinead, he knew he was wasting time in getting to his wife.

"What are you still doing on the phone Podge? Get over here now, I'm so scared and the pain is awful. I'm going to lose our baby, after all we planned it's going to be my fault and I'm so sore and there's lots of blood. It can't be good. Get over here, I'm so scared!"

"It's okay love, it'll be okay, I'm on my way and it'll all be okay, has Mary called an ambulance for you?"

Sinead told him she had and he hung up, continuing to his car. He had started moving almost as soon as he'd picked up on what was happening, so he was now in the car park. He jumped into the driver's seat and spun the tyres as he took off. He had to get to his wife, no Police, no driving rules would stop him. 'Why did I tell her everything is going to be ok? I don't know that, in fact I know that's the opposite of how this is going to end. We've lost our child, the one we've planned for and waited for. At least the doctors will set Sinead straight about her diet and I bet Mary had her working in the stores too. If only she had listened to me when I told her to be careful and look after herself.'

Padraig's mind raced as quickly as he sped through the town. Two secondary school children on the hop, managed to jump out of his way as he broke the pedestrian lights but for all his speed the ambulance beat him. He was too late and had to run back to his car and chase the ambulance to the hospital.

When Padraig arrived at the hospital, Sinead had already been triaged and the ante-natal specialists had been called down from their department. Padraig burst through the curtains surrounding Sinead's trolley. She was all cried out and lay on her side facing the wall and away from Padraig. He moved to hold her hand but she pushed him away. She was sore and drained and felt incredibly guilty. She had lost their child and all she wanted was for her loving husband to take her in his arms and tell her everything was going to be okay. She wanted him to bring her through this awful time with his support. But she felt too guilty to allow this to happen and Padraig was too clueless to know better.

"I can't believe this has happened to us Sinead. Have they said anything about why this happened or what caused it? Was there anything else we could've done to stop it from happening?"

"You mean was there anything I could have done differently Padraig, don't you? Just fucking hold me will you? They said something about an ultrasound or something but I don't know, maybe Mary knows? She was listening better than me, where is she?"

"I told her to go home. I'm here now so there was no need for her to hang around."

"You did what? Why would you do that Padraig? She
looked after me so well, closed up the shop made sure
the paramedics looked after me. Why would you send
her away after all that? She's my best friend Padraig!"
"Sure you don't need her now I'm here. I can look after
you and we'll get the doctors to sort everything out for
you. In fact, they should be in here with you doing
something shouldn't they? Where are there all?"
Padraig pushed back through the cubicle curtain in a
flash and searched the corridor for the closest medical
professional. He left Sinead all alone in the quiet cubicle.
She was filled with a consuming anger, wondering why
this had happened to her. Why was Padraig worse than
useless? She was in so much pain, overwhelmed with
sadness and all she wanted was for him to step up and be
there for her. But he'd run out the door at the first
opportunity. Even if he'd let Mary stay she could've held
her hand while he went to search for her doctor. He
could be so insensitive at times. Here she was lying
broken in hospital, her dreams of motherhood cruelly
dashed for the time being and even still he couldn't bring
himself to hold her.
So often in the books she read and the films she watched
there were grand gestures and massive declarations of
love. For all that though, the real truth of the
relationships, at least in Sinead's opinion, was in the
small details and even in the clichés. Sometimes all she
wanted, all she needed, was for Padraig to be there and
to hold her, to have him fully present in the moment, for
him to enjoy their closeness and not be thinking and
planning for the future. He'd rabbit on about taking the
little one to the park, seeing them off to school and all

the rest. All the while Sinead had lain beside him, just seven weeks pregnant, praying to God that the tiny being inside her, in whom Padraig had already invested so much love, would be kept safe and well right through to the moment he/she was born. At least then the pressure Padraig heaped on her would be lessened and she wouldn't feel burdened by what should have been a positive and beautiful journey.

And yet God hadn't answered those prayers. He hadn't listened to Sinead on the quiet mornings she lay awake beside Padraig, wondering if the stress he was putting on her could have a detrimental effect on their dream of becoming parents.

So the nightmare had come to pass. Sinead lay in a cold hospital trolley all alone, feeling hollow and defeated. Her husband had chased away her best friend and then run off himself to try and find her doctor. She tried to curl up in a foetal position but cruel irony being what it is, she couldn't even do that. The pain in her abdomen was too much. Instead she turned on her side again, with her face to the wall and though she thought she had cried herself dry, the tears flowed freely once again. It wasn't meant to play out like this and yet God had let it happen and ignored all her prayers for protection and safety.

20.

A sharp whistle from the kettle on the hob pierced the silence of the kitchen. It was to go unheeded however. Sinead McGrath stood looking out over their garden, exactly an acre in size. This had been vitally important to them when choosing their new home. Plenty of bedrooms and lots of space to play were pre-requisites before they'd even look at a property.

So miniscule and petty these considerations felt to Sinead this morning. Eight days had passed since she had found herself in Longford general, losing her baby. At the beginning she had planned to return to work this morning but Mary knew the score and had insisted Sinead take as long as she needed to recover before she even considered returning to work.

So here she found herself, staring out over a space that looked too big and isolated, when just ten days ago it was perfect. Sinead had felt such sadness and loss for the first few days but over the weekend this began to change to anger. She searched for an answer to the question that would never be answered. She asked herself, she asked Padraig, she asked her parents, she asked the doctors but no one could answer her questions; why me? Why did this happen? What did I do to deserve this?

Nobody could answer these questions and the more times they said 'I don't know', the angrier she became. Sleep was impossible and even rest was beyond her. A mind racing with a thousand questions and thoughts at once is not easy to calm. Every time she closed her eyes, the words formed on the inside of her eyelids and screamed louder in her head, demanding her attention. After a week these questions joined together to form simply white noise, white noise that drowned out televisions, kettles and the sound of Padraig's voice. Sinead spent her days staring into the middle distance, making the odd cup of tea and slipping further and further into a pit of depression, sadness and guilt.

It was nice of Mary to have given her the time off but with Padraig back at work she felt more isolated and alone. She had no friends or family close by to stop in on her or talk to about the weather. Her parents had been on the phone a couple of times but when they had visited everything had been stilted and awkward. The pity her Mam showed was too much for Sinead to manage while her father came across as uncaring because he feared death and loss so much. He was afraid to say sorry, afraid to say the wrong thing and uncomfortable facing up to death and mortality.

Sinead took the kettle off the hob and returned to bed without her tea. She had barely eaten in a week. Her guilt at being alive and her child not suppressed her appetite completely, leaving her weaker and more tired. As she pulled the duvet close around her body and hugged her hot water bottle tight, Sinead could recognise she was stuck in a vicious cycle of depression and needed help. But where could she go for that?

Padraig kept sending the few people who knocked on the door away, telling them he can provide all the support she needs. Mary was doing what she thought best and giving her time and space, her parents were terrified of making things worse somehow. Then there was Padraig himself.

Everything he did now repulsed and infuriated her in a way she had never thought possible. Every single thing he said was wrong. Every time he breathed it was too loud. Every time he asked her was she ok, it angered her. Sinead had felt so lost and broken for over a week, why did he need to ask? Meanwhile in his wretched practicality he had already compartmentalised what they'd been through.

Despite going missing looking for a doctor he had stayed beside her until she was released from the hospital. He had even brought her home ever so delicately. It was reminiscent of their earliest days together; he was attentive and couldn't do enough for Sinead. But when he returned to work everything changed again.

He was awake and gone that morning before Sinead woke from a fitful sleep. They had fallen asleep in each other's arms, two scared and sad people dragging themselves through hell as a couple. And yet just 9 hours later Sinead awoke alone, cold and with a massive feeling of loss. She wished she could have woken in Padraig's comforting arms.

Then it her like a train. Surprisingly, she had forgotten, even if it had been just for millisecond. Her child was gone.

Two days before she had woken up with her child inside her and their futures lay out before them. Today, she lay in bed alone, not even her growing child for company, all their hopes and dreams dashed and in a million pieces. With her husband having snuck out to work without even saying goodbye. This was a crash of thunder that exploded in her heart. She cried until she thought it impossible to cry any more, she swore and cursed at God while begging and wishing to change the story but despite it all, it was all in vain.

Padraig had continued about his routine after what had been, in his mind, a speed-bump on their way to a full house and a perfect family. Two days after the miscarriage he had accompanied Sinead on her follow-up appointment. But in Sinead's mind he couldn't have been listening to the same conversation because on the way home he had merely said, 'it's alright love, we can always try again soon. You'll be fine again and then we can start our family. We'll just have to be even more careful the next time and make sure we don't do the wrong thing.'

Sinead was still in shock and was unable to do anything but nod in agreement with anything he said. She just wanted to get home and try to process all the emotional and hormonal changes she'd been through all week. Later as she lay in bed trying to piece her broken heart together again, she heard Padraig's words for the first time. She heard the sub-text and the implications behind his words. She heard what Padraig really felt.

Padraig blamed her for the miscarriage. He was angry at her and felt that she must have done something wrong that brought on their loss. He may have said 'we' need to be more careful and 'we' can't do anything wrong but what could actually do at this early stage of her pregnancy?

So his language had betrayed him. It was hard enough dealing with her physical and emotional stress without learning of Padraig's anger at her and disbelief at what had happened. 'Is he right? Is it my fault?' she continuously asked herself.

Later that day she gave Mary a quick call in the shop. She didn't like leaving Mary on her own in the shop but she wasn't ready to be working with the public. She couldn't hold Mary up for long, if Mary could even answer the phone at all. So when Mary did answer the phone she simply blurted out her question.

"Is it my fault I miscarried?" Mary was quick to answer the phone and luckily there wasn't anyone in the shop but she was still taken aback by Sinead's question.

"Of course it wasn't your fault honey, why would you even think that?"

"It was something Padraig said to me about not making the same mistakes again next time I'm pregnant."

"What's he on about 'next time you're pregnant?' you need to recover your strength and deal with your loss first. Was he talking about you working in the stores and not getting enough nutrition?"

"No it was nothing specific he said, just that we'd have to learn, why did he say something to you about those things?"

"It was just something he mentioned when I called him last week. He wanted to know where you were when you first felt ill and if you'd be listening to him about caffeine and your diet."

"He's a fucking prick!" Sinead's language surprised Mary who was used to Sinead's more reserved mannerisms. "The fucking dickhead hears I'm probably miscarrying and the first thing he thinks is what have I done to bring it on? He's been smothering me with attention for weeks but he's barely looked at me since

Thursday. He just saw me as a fucking incubator for his child! And now I've lost it he must be angry and bitter at me."

Mary didn't like Padraig, never had really. He was always demanding attention and was full of his own self-importance. She considered stepping in to lessen the damage to Padraig but only for a split-second. Instead she just followed up with, "he was pissing me off with all the phone-calls to you here and I got the impression he felt that you should be taking to your bed like a woman from the '50s. He would give out if I told him you were in the stores, 'she shouldn't be working there in her condition', as if you were a china doll or something."

"I used to love how much attention he paid me and wanted to protect me. But lately it's been like he doesn't want me to have a life of my own, to merely be the mother to his children. Why can't he just hold me and tell me everything will be ok instead of ignoring and blaming me?"

Sinead's question wasn't meant to be rhetorical but Mary could think of no good answer and stayed quiet. Sinead herself was beginning to reassess everything about their relationship up to that point. But that was a thread that couldn't be stopped once she started pulling at it.

21.

Their love for each other was razed to the ground in no time. Feelings soured quickly and their anger and bitterness grew harder by the day. Sinead challenged Padraig about his thoughts on the miscarriage being her fault but wasn't comforted in any way by his responses. He did try to sound reassuring but Sinead knew, when he wouldn't meet her gaze; that he didn't believe in his own words. He had always been an easy man to read and he couldn't lie to save his life.

This had come in handy on the rare occasions Sinead had been forced to check his story. It also meant that when he told her he loved and cherished every day they were together, Sinead could trust in it completely. And yet this self-same character trait she had loved about him now grated with a fury she could scarcely believe. He had returned to work so quickly that they never grieved together, even though grieving was what she needed most. Padraig meanwhile didn't feel the same and had moved on to thoughts of their next try within a couple of days.

He didn't recognise the need to see past his own thoughts to the woman he loved. Sinead knew he still did love her but their lives had changed drastically. He was angry as he felt Sinead must be in some way partially to blame, while she resented Padraig's ability to move on so quickly and get back to normal. Meanwhile she tried to sleep off her incredible fatigue and cry every last tear she could before returning to work.

When she did Mary supported and watched out for her in ways Padraig didn't. She sensed when something was wrong and pre-empted it. All without smothering her like Padraig did. Padraig's reticence and irritability contrasted markedly with Mary's support and comfort. Once Sinead felt Padraig's blame she began questioning everything about them as a couple.

She wanted to pick herself up and try again, and she knew many women did and do, but it was the lack of a grieving process that hurt the most. If Padraig had only spoken to her and grieved alongside her things might have been different. But because he barely shed a tear and felt no great loss for something they barely had, Sinead saw him as a cold, calculating character rather than the gentle, caring man she had fallen for. When Mary had let slip about Padraig's reaction to her phone-call, Sinead was tempted to drop him immediately. She knew his caring sometimes strayed into smothering but when he questioned her role in the miscarriage she felt betrayed.

"Sometimes accidents happen Sinead and they are nobody's fault. No matter what we do or the precautions we take, there are still accidents all around the world all the time. Some are massive physically and some are big emotionally. They still happen and even with all the health and safety precautions sometimes we just can't explain them. I've lost count how many times I've told you this Sinead but I'll continue to until you believe me."

Gradually Mary's advice began to sink in for Sinead and she decided she had to talk to Padraig about everything.

Maybe it was just a coping mechanism he was using.
Mary meanwhile was continuing.
"You know I've never been his biggest fan,
understatement I know! But this is a very emotional time
for both of you, even if he is denying his emotions at the
moment. It's not the time to be having a go at each other
or making snap decisions. You both need to find a way
to communicate better or you'll never find a way
through."
The McGraths couldn't sustain their love and happiness
together. The trust, bond and love they had built up
slowly until they knew each other better than themselves,
eroded quickly following their vastly different reactions
to what had been a traumatic event leading to lots of
guilt and depression for Sinead. They argued constantly
when before they had never exchanged a cross word.
They were short, irritable and became two individuals
sharing a house that was too big and echoed with the
reminders of their loss.
Sinead made a big effort to control her anger and find
some sort of common ground between them. But Padraig
pushed her away just when she needed him most.
"Accidents don't just happen like that Sinead, if you'd
had a car crash or fallen that would have been something
to blame but to have a baby one day and not the next
makes no sense. There needs to be a cause, were you
overdoing it in work or not managing the diet that added
stress to your body?"
"Or maybe it was you calling the shop every five
minutes that added the stress!" For days she bit her
tongue but Sinead finally blurted it out to Padraig. The
same argument over and over and trying to reason had

left their mark on Sinead. She had some residual pain, wasn't sleeping right and she was barely functioning so she had wanted to punish him for the guilt he was making her feel.

Sinead regretted her words as soon as they were out of her mouth. She was still in love with the man before her and didn't really want to intentionally hurt him. Now she felt guilty for that too. Her mind had been beating her up for so long she hadn't the energy to fight her emotions anymore. No matter how much Mary disagreed and told her she was wrong, no matter how many doctors, and nurses told her she'd done nothing wrong, she believed completely that she was being punished for something she had done wrong. She accepted all the guilt, even over spat out insults, like it was something she deserved. The McGrath's passed each other in their house; it was too big and too empty to still be there home. They barely spoke, they never touched and they never even smiled. They were two zombies trapped in purgatory. Padraig worked all the hours God gave until he returned home exhausted, slept and returned to work early the next day. When he left for work and Sinead would drag herself to the shower. She would make it to the shop, at least for a couple of hours, tidy the storeroom a little and price a few items. Every so often she would feel up to serving a customer or two and doing what she did so well which was selling. This could go well but a mother pushing a buggy into the shop could bring about a collapse in Sinead's defensive walls.

"Take yourself away home Sin, we can go again tomorrow but will you please talk to Padraig again or make an appointment with your GP. I hate seeing you like this and whatever you're doing isn't working. I need my friend back, I need my partner back, I can't sell snow to the Eskimos like you can!" Mary tried to lighten the mood but there was truth behind her words. Mary could manage and run the business but Sinead made the big sales, she had whatever it was that was necessary to make people part with their cash.

For Sinead and Padraig the next 15-20 years had been mapped out and no decisions were taken, whether on a house, a job or spending money, without thinking how it fit into the plans. It wasn't necessarily the most romantic and spontaneous set-up but having been together since they were teenagers they were happy with it. They were each other's first kiss and after splitting after school to find themselves, for two weeks, they had settled down together.

When their friends invited one or other they knew both would turn up. They lived in each other's pocket and were incredibly close and always planning for their future together. They started saving for their home while still in college. Theirs was not a puppy love or a love based on teenage urges like their friends, they had a bond and companionship beyond their years. If they decided to do something, it happened. There was never a setback on their journey. That was until the miscarriage.

They didn't have the coping skills between them to deal with something going wrong. No plan could protect them from the frustration, anger and guilt they felt over what had befallen them. So when Sinead descended the stairs at 10pm she was filled with an emotion she wasn't used to or prepared for. Mary had sent her home yet again but she knew without doubt that she needed to find a way through alone. Padraig just didn't have the coping skills to help her.

Deep down she knew he lacked the emotional maturity to deal with the torment visited on them. He would continue to throw himself into work, hoping that with enough money and stuff for their house they would overcome. So Sinead steeled herself for a conversation she never could have imagined before. It would be traumatic and difficult in its' own way but it was necessary.

Padraig would be staying in work late, hopeful of sneaking into bed while Sinead fell asleep in front of the television again but Sinead would be ready for his arrival tonight. The age it took him to negotiate the one lock on the hall door and then to enter the living room persuaded Sinead he hadn't been in the office all evening.

"You decided to come home at last then? How many pints did you force Dave to sit through before you let him off home to his girlfriend? By the slow entry into the house and the brewery smell I'd imagine it was more than one or two, yeah?" No answer was necessary as he groped about for the armchair and eventually collapsed into the seat. In spite of his condition, Sinead was determined to follow through and have this conversation. "Was Dave with you at all or were you drinking on your own again, like an old man or an alcoholic?"

"Dave was there for a couple and so was Richard but neither of them could stay and they went home to their girls!"

"You forget I know you better than anyone and before the miscarriage you would have been the one coming home to me for a cuddle instead of being in the pub and you never saw it as a bad thing. I was all you needed, but in the last few weeks you've gone to any lengths to avoid spending time with me and you're drinking like a fish. It wasn't my fucking fault! It could have happened to anyone, anytime. You have to get that through your head or we'll never be able to carry on together."

The bombshell hit Padraig right between the eyes. He had been so lost in work and boozing, he had presumed they were just coping in different ways. Couples went through difficulties but they'd get over the miscarriage and have lots of children, or so he thought. Never had he imagined that Sinead could have thought differently.

"Listen to me Padraig, I've spoken to all the professionals and anyone else who might have an opinion and they've all told me we were unlucky for reasons unknown but it's been made worse by how we've reacted. I'm heartbroken and I'm going to cry and release my emotions and then at some point I'll move on. But you? What have you done? I presume you're just as upset but you've thrown yourself into work and the pub and I don't recognise you anymore. You always had time for me but now you avoid me, you never talk to me and you drink more than I ever saw you do before. Do you even love or care for me still?"

All Padraig had to do was lie. He could've said of course I still love you and we'll get through this. But Padraig couldn't lie.

"Right now I don't think so Sinead. You lost our first child, the one we've planned since we were teenagers." Days spent thinking about this conversation and hours preparing for it were distilled into one line for Sinead. The reality of how he really felt was laid out before her and there was no more strength, no more energy, and no more words.

Eventually Sinead spoke, a whisper full of venom and anger. "You're an absolute prick Podge! You're trying to make me feel bad over something I had no control over. I thought I knew you better than even myself but I hate the man sitting before me tonight. Even when all you need to say is you love me, you don't, and you can't get passed blaming me. And I blame myself enough than to take on your blame too."

22.

Sunday morning rolled around as it tends to do. Maura was off at Mass and the kids were sleeping off last nights' pints and shots. Paul had the house to himself and it had been a long week. His head was all over the place and he actually appreciated the kids and Maura leaving him alone with his thoughts, or lack of them.

"C'mon Rust and we'll get our constitutional in." His faithful dog ambled up to the back door from his kennel. Stepping out of his kennel Rusty threw his eyes to the heavens and then at Paul. The rain was fine and misty and Paul could see the question forming in Rustys' mind. 'Are you kidding me old man? I'm too old to be going out in this feckin' rain!'

"I know Rusty, I know it's a horrible morning but as Billy says 'there's no such thing as bad weather only the wrong clothes!' and sure our arthritic joints could probably do with the stroll and the lubrication." Again Paul looked in his dogs' eyes as he put on the lead and felt he could read his mind again.

"I know I use that line too much but it doesn't make it any less true." Paul and Rusty wandered towards the front door together and Paul went to put on the alarm. Two numbers in he remembered it was Sunday, the kids were still in bed and if they moved at all they would set off the alarm.

"Lucky I remembered eh Rusty?" Responding to his name like he'd done for 15 years, Rusty looked up at Paul. "How come I know exactly what you are thinking and what you are going to do but I can't get into the heads of those two kids upstairs? We don't know each other, we rarely spend time together and I've no real rapport with them have I?" Paul pulled the door shut behind him, quietly so as to let his two children sleep but it was too late.

As Paul and Rusty ambled down the garden to the front gate they left Jack crouching on the landing. On the way back to bed after a quick piss-stop he had heard everything his Dad had just said to the dog. 'Is it any wonder we never want to disturb him with our lives and what's going on for us?' Jack thought as he returned to his room.

****

Paul had no pace or determination in his walk this morning. Even Rusty was able to keep up with him this morning and found he was getting ahead of Paul, almost having to wait for him at times. Subconsciously Paul knew that every step he took and every second that went by brought him closer to his return to The Local and seeing Charlie after a week. The first time would always be difficult and he was kicking himself for not getting it over with during the week. The longer the week went on, the more embarrassed he felt at last Sundays' action. And he knew that Derek being Derek he'd be there trying to wind him up. But being a creature of habit Paul knew exactly where he would be at 12.31 on a Sunday afternoon.

As he and Rusty rounded the corner from Beach Road onto Dublin Street, he put the lead back on Rusty. A kinder, gentler dog you would never find but Paul knew all about the wrath of the dog gestapo and always held Rusty on his lead through the town.

"Another great day for a stroll, eh Paul?" The dog walker pointed out helpfully as Paul bent to put on the lead. "No fucking shit Sherlock!" he replied to his chest before managing a fake smile as he glanced up at the dog walker. His acting skills must have been better than he thought because the man took it as a joke, not an insult, and chuckled to himself at the wit as he carried on down the road.

"That guy's a fucking strange fish isn't he Rusty? Even when you take the piss, he just laughs it off and carries on!" Paul glanced at his watch and realised he was behind where he normally would be by this hour. "Come on horse, we need to put the boot down if we're to be sitting under the willow tree before Fr. Murphy lets Maura and the rest of the congregation out on good behaviour."

For the first time all morning, Paul began to stride out in his familiar manner and at his usual pace. Rusty was beginning to get dragged along quicker than he would really have wanted. Paul wasn't looking forward to walking back into The Local but at the same time he knew within a couple of minutes he'd have a pint in front of him.

The newspaper man outside St. Peters is a good talker, a salesman after all, but he couldn't coax a word out of Paul this particular morning. It only took a few seconds but he managed to mention the weather, the dog and the latest inner-city murder but none could illicit more than a grunt from Paul. Maura wasn't to have any more joy in her efforts to talk to her husband.

"Here!" was all Paul said as he thrust Rusty's lead and the newspaper in Maura's direction. She was barely off the front steps of the Church before Paul had left the shade of the willow tree to do this. She was embarrassed by the looks she could see and the tuts she could hear from her fellow mass-goers. She was desperate to make any connection with Paul to show them they were alright, despite Paul's anger at her.

"I'll have your dinner on the table for half 2 ok love?" She didn't expect him to say much, even a smile would have done but Paul just turned on his heel and marched off towards The Local. From the open, discursive man of last Monday night, Paul had retreated to the sullen, cold and gruff character he had grown in to.

She had hoped he had appreciated talking and crying together and that maybe that would turn over a new leaf in him of openness. Maybe even he would be in a position to deal with his emotions. Sadly this wasn't to be and her heart broke a little more as Paul marched off to his place of Sunday worship. A place where bravado and bluster were revered more than confessing to having emotions of any kind.

****

Two things in particular come very difficultly to proud, old-school men; and Paul was no different. He hated having to apologise for anything and he did everything in his power to avoid asking for help or admitting to not coping with whatever life threw at him.

With that in mind he stopped himself just as he reached the pub door. "Come on, you've put this off long enough. Take a deep breath, apologise to Charlie and then enjoy your couple of pints before dinner."

So taking a very conscious deep breath he pushed open the door and entered The Local. Quicker than an undercover MI5 agent he scanned the pub for signs of life. Two fresh pints of lager on the counter meant two customers was the full extent of custom. 'Still no sign of Brian back in his seat by the door either' thought Paul. 'Poor fella must be still in the depths of it all.'

He spotted Derek over at the fruit machine which accounted for one pint, leaving just one customer to identify. Derek made some smart-arse comment about Rocky Balboa but he was very easy to ignore. Instead Paul made his way to the top of the pub and hung his coat on the stand.

"Thought I heard a voice alright" said Charlie, emerging from behind the counter. "Will I put you on a pint?"

"Yeah Charlie, that'd be great…… please" he added almost as an afterthought as he climbed onto his stool.

"Please Pauly? Fucking hell what's going on? A barmaid would think you were on your best behaviour, has something happened?" Charlie asked; her voice laced with sarcasm. She was enjoying having a little power over Paul for a change and relished the chance to make him squirm.

"Come on Charlie, you know full well why I haven't seen you all week and…. Eh… yeah… you know I am, don't you?"

"I know you are what Mr Forsyth? Have you been helping yourself to Fr. Murphy's communion wine this morning? You're talking in bloody riddles!"

"You know I'm sorry is what I mean. It's not easy to say and I was embarrassed by last Sundays' goings on. It was stupid."

"I know you are Paul. I've already forgotten about it. Just do the same and we'll be fine." Charlie placed his pint in front of him and picked up his fiver to take for the pint. As she placed the coins beside his pint, Paul gave her a nod of gratitude. He then turned the glass until the harp faced him square on. With a gentle touch he began methodically removing the condensation from his glass. Charlie could see the edges of his mouth moving as he mouthed his silent words before taking his first sip.

'Here's to you son. I'm sorry for everything and losing our photo but I'll get another one from the box to replace it. You know I don't need one to remember you but I like having you close all the time. So I drink this pint to you James and I will do with every pint I take until we meet again.'

Paul took a long pull on his pint. The first one always tastes nice but having been in exile for a time, Paul was savouring every drop. He sat with both palms flat on the counter, either side of his pint and merely stared into the darkness of his pint and the creaminess of its head. He sat; relieved and contented to be back in his spot and ready to move on.

But he wouldn't be allowed to just yet.

23.

Replacing stock in the empty fridges Charlie jumped
suddenly to her feet. "Fuck it Charlie I nearly knocked
me pint over!" Paul blurted and he even caught Derek's
shoulders twitch a little at the noise. 'He must be on a
roll though' he thought 'because he's not turning away
from that screen to check out the commotion.
Ignoring Paul and his early morning profanity, Charlie
made for the staff noticeboard out of sight of the bar. She
returned to the counter moments later with a square of
paper in her hand.
"I found this last weekend when I was cleaning up Paul.
I'm sure it's important to someone, maybe you'd
recognise who might own it?"
"What is it a betting slip? Cash the fucking thing and
we'll have a session!"
"Calm yourself old man, it's not a betting slip. I've
asked everyone this week so I think you're about the
only person I haven't seen to ask. I know your Jack has
dark hair but maybe you know whose lad this is?"
Paul nearly choked on his pint, had a heart attack and a
stroke all at the same time. He had spent 24 years hiding
his deepest secret. But know, here he was, confronted in
his spiritual home with a photo of his beautiful boy
James.
There he was, all blonde curls and happiness, smiling at
him from Charlie's hand. A tsunami of emotions washed
over him and he was grateful to be sitting down. He was
happy to see James and delighted to have his favourite
photo back. He was disgusted that Charlie had found it.

Relieved that Charlie had found it. Ashamed he had lied to so many people for so long. Guilty about his part in James' death. Angry at being unable to conceal all these emotions playing out on his face as Charlie just stood there holding the photograph before him. In an instant his life and his relationship with his pint-time confessor had changed irrevocably.

Charlie stood in shock staring at Paul and wondering about his reaction. She had imagined he might have recognised one of his drinking buddies' grandchildren in the photo but this was so much more. The stoic, sharp man who never showed emotion, good or bad, was crumbling right before he eyes. Yes she could see him trying in vain to regain some composure but it was too late. This photo undoubtedly was of vital importance to Paul and was stirring up deep emotions in a man she knew but certainly not as a friend.

'Should I go around and sit with him? Should I lean on the counter and talk to him? Should I tell the other 2 customers to fuck off and lock the door behind them?' There is no manual for bar work and even if there were, this situation would not be included. All these thoughts ran around her head in seconds just like Paul 2 yards away. The only physical contact she'd ever had with Paul was when their hands touched exchanging money. She is no touchy feely person and Paul was definitely too old-school for that carry-on. Normally.

Even the thought of shaking hands could turn Paul away. In spite of all this, Charlie had seen through the façade to the vulnerable man beneath. He was instantly older and more drawn than he had ever looked before. She wondered about walking around to sit beside him and comfort him.

Instead she sat herself up onto the fridge opposite Pauls' chair and pushed a serviette across the counter to him.

"I don't fucking need that Charlie, I'm no fucking crier." Paul whispered. The anger was there but it wasn't backed up by any energy.

"You say that Paul but I can see the tears and don't worry I'll keep my mouth shut about them too. But how would you feel if Derek over there saw them or somebody else was to walk in and see you crying?" Reluctantly Paul leant forward picked up the serviette and dabbed delicately at the corner of his eyes. "Where did you find that photo?" he asked from behind his mask. It was all that he could think of and he was barely able to say the words.

Having strained to hear him, Charlie replied in a whisper "last Sunday night. We were sweeping the floors and one of the lounge boys saw it. He picked it up and gave it to me. I thought it might be yours and it had fallen out of your wallet last Sunday. Remember I handed it back to you after… you know? But when I saw the blonde curls I presumed it wasn't yours, what with Jack being so dark haired. That's why I just shoved it at you without warning; I thought you might recognise somebody else's grandchild. I take it you know exactly who it is now though?"

Paul picked up the small photo of his little treasure and without looking away from his eyes replied"this is my little boy James…… it was taken on June 11th, 1990……… the day he……… the day he died."

For 24 long and torturous years Maura and Paul had kept the secret of their loss from all the people they knew. Twenty years of denying, lying and avoiding grieving correctly and the first person, the first fucking person, Paul confesses all to is Charlie, the barmaid in The Local.

****

After 12 years working at the counter of The Local, Charlie had presumed she'd heard it all. She knew about the affairs, she knew about the divorces, the kids in trouble and the rest. She never had to try to overhear plenty of gossip, rumour and innuendo.

But Paul's words didn't seem to be registering with her. 'Did he just tell me he lost a son in 1990? The same day Ireland played England in the World Cup? 'It IS possible I suppose? How could someone keep that secret for so long? But then again none of us know anything about the Forsyth's from before they moved into the area.'

Charlie realised she hadn't said anything to Paul since his revelation and from somewhere came a plan of action. "Fuck me Paul, that's an awful lot to take in on a Sunday morning" she began "but we certainly can't leave it there so here's what we'll do. You go for a piss, a cry or whatever in the gents and I'll distract Derek with a pint and a couple of quid for the machine and then I'll be back for a chat. I don't know what I can do but it might help to unburden yourself and have someone listen to your story."

With that she moved and she was gone with a determined stride. "Here you go young man!" she said, appearing at Derek's shoulder. He'd been so stuck into his game he hadn't noticed her approaching. "I'm always so hard on you so here have a pint by way of making up. Lots of bells and whistles going off this morning, you up by much?"

"Yeah a decent bit. Somebody must have fed a fortune into losing last night because I'm winning every pull."

"Good stuff, well just in case your luck turns, here's a couple of quid to soften the blow and keep playing with."

"Thanks sweet cheeks!" Derek replied, slapping her arse for good measure. Normally Charlie would have railed on him but this wasn't the time. 'Bigger fish to fry Charlene, how are you going to begin this conversation with Paul?' She was still thinking this as she bolted the front door as quietly as she could, hoping Derek couldn't see her behind the porch walls. She knew she'd hear Derek moving, the other customer had disappeared mid-pint and she didn't want anyone else to distract her.

Paul was already sitting on his stool by the time Charlie got back behind the counter. 'Where in the hell do I start this conversation?' he thought to himself. 'I've never wanted to tell anyone about James but now it's out I better tell Charlie the lot.' If only he could mind-read he'd know Charlie was just as uneasy as he was about the coming conversation.

Picking up her coffee, Charlie moved to the end of the counter and sat down close to Paul. "I don't know where to start Paul. I've no idea what you want to tell me or what I can possibly say in reply. But even considering all that I'd prefer you to share the story with me instead of any of the customers in here, at least you know anything you tell me will stay between the two of us.

"Jaysus Charlie if I had the choice I'd be saying nothing at all to anyone, just like I've done for 24 years."

"Just tell me as much or as little as you like."

"Right, well you know we only moved here in '91. I've been drinking here ever since and Maura's been in here once a year, at Christmas, with me. We only moved here when living in Rush became too tough. My little boy James was born in 1987. We were only kids, too young to be parents. It cuts me up to this day but I didn't want a child, I wasn't ready to be a father.

Neither of us have any family so we were all alone, left to try and cope. I can't believe I'm going to say this out loud but I spent many nights while Maura was pregnant hoping something might happen."

24.

Charlie looked up to see if Paul had really meant what he had just said. Had he really wished for Maura to have a miscarriage? He, meanwhile, had picked a spot on the floor to focus on.

"You mean a miscarriage Paul? You prayed for a miscarriage?" Charlie made no effort to mask the judgement in her voice.

"I've always felt guilty for it but yes I thought at the time it might have been the right thing to happen for us. But please believe me I do regret that and I feel so guilty for wishing it on Maura."

Charlie shook her head and bit her tongue. This was more out of shock than any decision on her part.

"Anyway James was born happy and healthy. I was young, I didn't know what to do but when I saw that boy smile at me I felt even guiltier for what I'd thought. In an instant my mind changed and I was excited to be a father and we'd be ok. I did everything wrong though. I made loads of mistakes but I was enthusiastic and Maura had no idea of what I'd thought while she was pregnant. But despite all my good intentions I struggled to do the right things when I was with James on my own. But on June 11th, 1990 I came home from work and insisted on taking James to the park on my own. Everyone was talking about the football and I just wanted to get out in the air. I was trying to force a bond to grow before it had chance to form naturally.

I hadn't accepted that he was going to be a part of our life right up until he was born. But within a few weeks

I'd fallen in love with my little lad even though I was hopeless and clueless. I couldn't read him like Maura could, I couldn't find out what was wrong with him. She was breastfeeding him too so I never got a look in. As soon as he could he made straight for Maura all the time. My boy was ignoring me in favour of Maura and I convinced myself it was because he knew what I'd been thinking."

"That you wanted Maura to miscarry?"

"Exactly Charlie."

"Well it wasn't a good thought to have, especially when so many people want to have children and can't get pregnant or have miscarriages."

"I know, I know" Paul said "it's been bothering me for years."

"But did you ever say anything out loud? Did you ever say it in front of anyone who was pregnant?"

"No, no, not at all. I can't even remember whether it was a thought I had for minutes, days or weeks. The guilt from those thoughts is wrapped up in the guilt of what happened in Castle Park. I left his side for half a second, I swear. I went back to get his coat and hat and he was gone. He ran out of the playground, I think I'd promised him a treat at home so he was sprinting, as fast as his little legs could, to get to the car. He must have tripped up over his own legs or on the edge of the path……….

"Paul?"

"That was when I heard it. I didn't know but knew what it was all at the same time. I was just rounding the corner when I saw him. His face looking serene but there was so much blood. It was at the back of his head and on the kerb beneath him."

Charlie couldn't speak. She daren't. Paul was in full flow and she didn't want to interrupt him despite all the questions in her mind.

"The next 24 hours are still a blur to me, especially after all these years. In fact there's a lot of the next week or so that I don't remember. I was on some sort of auto-pilot and felt like I had to be strong for Maura and just carry on."

"Jesus Paul that's awful for you both, did you even let yourself cry at all or grieve? Could you feel anything? How did Maura feel?"

"I definitely didn't cry, I never wanted to show my pain in front of Maura. I didn't grieve I don't think, not in any proper way anyway. I think I just closed down that part of my brain."

"But you must have felt so bad? Did you not even let your emotions out when you were on your own?"

"Anger was the dominant feeling I think and I felt incredibly guilty and was constantly berating myself."

"But it must have been such a sad time for you and all you felt was guilt and anger?"

"I blamed myself Charlie, I still do"

"But it was an accident Paul?"

"That's what Maura said to me the other day too but it doesn't stop the guilt. I was on my own with James when it happened. I shouldn't have let him run off on his own. It was a fucking hat and coat, why were they so important? If I'd just left them he wouldn't have been running alone. I also felt I was being punished for what I'd thought during the pregnancy. So that added more guilt and anger to the fires of hell I was in. I was angry at God or whoever for putting that pain on Maura and on

James. They'd done nothing wrong and were being
punished so I felt really guilty for that. Then there's the
thing I'm most ashamed of."
"What?"
"I was angry at them too"
"Angry at who?"
"I was angry at James and Maura. I blamed Maura for
making a fuss over the jacket and hat before I left the
house and meaning I left him alone. But worst of all, I
blamed James too. I blamed my sweet little lad."
Charlie had tears beginning in the corner of her eyes. She
was glad to have locked the door and no one else could
see what was going on. Paul meanwhile lifted James'
photo in front of his face and brought his gaze from the
floor to his son.
"I'm so sorry son but it's true I blamed you for being
young. I blamed you for not waiting for me. I blamed
you for running instead of walking on the uneven path. I
blamed you for leaving your mother heartbroken. I
blamed you for showing me what true unconditional love
is and then ripping it away from me.
I loved you son, I mean I love you J but I've blamed you
and been angry at you for so long. You were just a child,
it's my responsibility. I should've known better and I
should have protected you better."
Charlie was struggling to take in all that Paul had
revealed. But despite her cold mannerisms and
demeanour at times she couldn't help but be touched by
Paul's revelations. She instinctively reached out for
Paul's hand which was still holding James' picture
before his eyes.

Paul pulled his hand away, leaving Charlie feeling somewhat foolish. Paul was angry that Charlie had coaxed these confessions from him with James' photo and he was angry at himself for spilling everything in one go. But Charlie was tough enough and smart enough to realise his first rebuff was just male pride and she wouldn't leave him.

"Don't try and push me away now that you've told me all this" she began. "You needed to talk about that and I've no idea how you've managed to keep that to yourself for so long. Sure I know everybody's business around here and yet you managed to keep THAT from me!" Charlie was trying to add a bit of humour to what was an impossible situation. "Here I was thinking you were cold-hearted and unfeeling but I suppose you've good reason for that."

"I can't believe I've opened up about all this to you Charlie but the last few weeks have been stirring up stuff all over the place. I could only keep the plates spinning for so long and then when you showed me the photograph the dam finally burst."

"But fucking hell I could've brought things to a head a little less jarringly than just shoving the photo in your face! If I'd had any idea Paul I would've been a little more sensitive. We've all got things we'd like to forget and never talk about but the world doesn't work that way does it?"

25.

"So with all that has happened recently, to Paddy and his family, this must've been rolling around your mind and fucking eating you up Paul?"

"Ah absolutely Charlie as soon as I heard what had happened I was back in 1990 myself. I remembered everything I've gone through; the guilt, the grief, the pain, the lot, it was like it was happening again but it was so real it felt like it was happening for the first time too?"

"What do you mean Paul?"

"When I went to the house and then to the church for the funeral I saw how numb all the family were. I spoke to Brian but his eyes were glazed over like he was on auto-pilot and when I noticed that I recognized it from myself all those years before."

"So you were really able to empathise with him?"

"Yeah of course, but it wasn't just that. I had been so numb I never let myself feel the emotions I was going through. So when I was watching Brian and his family I felt like James' death was happening at the same time. I wasn't just reliving it; it felt like the first time because I hadn't allowed myself to feel anything in 1990. It was so raw, it was harrowing and it felt so fucking real. For jaysus sake, on the Wednesday morning I had to stop myself touching the coffin as I came down from Communion. I had myself convinced it was James in the little white coffin before the altar."

"Fucking hell Paul, I can't imagine how that must feel, to feel like you've lost your child." Charlie's reply was immediate and she wondered for a second about when the lying had become so easy. 'Paul is breaking down in front of you and all he wants is a little comfort and someone to understand. Why can't you be the one to step up for him?'

But Paul was ploughing on, unaware of Charlene's inner monologue. " It's just that it was so similar, here was a father supposed to be looking out for their child on their own and then their child dies because of a horror accident. The guilt that poor man must be feeling is beyond comprehension. I mean he'll be torturing himself and second-guessing himself. I feel so guilty about what happened to James and what that did to Maura. I don't know Brian's missus but whether she carries any blame in her heart or not won't matter to Brian. He'll be beating himself up about this for years and years."

"Is that what you've done all these years Paul? Have you borne it all on your own shoulders?"

"Pretty much, yeah. I don't want to speak to Maura about it in any detail because I don't want to upset her. I don't like upsetting myself and I've always been afraid to open the dam in case it doesn't close again afterwards."

"But this can't be the right way either can it? Confessing to having any emotions, never mind difficult ones, to your barmaid over a pint? Jesus what sort of a position have you put me in? I don't know how to deal with this; I don't know how to respond. Fucking hell we all have our shit but there's got to be a professional who can help you out?"

"I don't know if I could do that Charlie, with a stranger, you know, just put myself completely out there for them to examine."

"For fucks sake Paul, you just did that to me! Fuck me" Charlie said, laughing at the contradiction, happy to laugh at anything, happy to release a little tension. "Jesus Paul" Charlene continued still laughing "Jesus I'll get myself a job up at the church. The confessions can't be as tough to listen to. Give me 10 Hail Mary's for staring at the neighbours tits any day!"

Paul began to chuckle now too. "Yeah you're right, I didn't mean to unload that on you in one go but it's about time I did and got things off my chest. I'll just find a more appropriate place to do it next time! Although you're cheaper than any counsellor and you'll let me drink during sessions!"

"Yeah but why couldn't you have kept to the pleasantries Paul. No religion, no politics, no fuck all serious belongs in a pub. Just leave me to pull the pints, talk shite about football and serve the punters…. Jesus the fucking customers!" With that Charlene was gone and running out from the counter to open the doors and let the thirsty masses in. She needn't have bothered. Two old fuckers smoking their pipes was the rush.

"Bloody hell Charlene, are you on a go-slow? I'm drier than the desert out here. Was it a good session last night had you down the cellar recovering?" Jimmy was laughing to himself as he pushed past Charlie and on to his seat at the counter. He couldn't give a damn why the doors were locked; he just enjoyed the opportunity of taking the piss.

"Oh, oh Paul you were in here with Charlene all alone with the door locked?!" Jimmy was in his element now as Paul emerged from the bathrooms after composing himself. "You know that's how rumours start in a small town don't you?!"

"What would Charlene be doing anywhere near this old timer? No she was just taking my confession, 10 Hail Mary's for me." Paul replied winking at Charlie having regained his more natural demeanour.

"Were you spying on Mrs. Potts sunbathing in her garden again? Jesus I'd take 10 Hail Marys for that chance! Come on Charlie throw me on a pint. Actually make it two, standing out there built up me thirst and I've some catching up to do!"

26.

"Don't be so fucking sure of yourself Charlene. You and
I have a history that goes way back. You forget I know
things that you definitely don't want to spread around the
town. Everyone knows you're a hard ass, or thinks that's
the way you are anyway. They'd be crushed and so
judgmental if they knew the truth wouldn't they?"
"Jesus Derek we were only fucking kids. We didn't
know any better and you didn't leave me much choice
when you fucked off to Scotland did you? That was
some mature response out of you wasn't it?"
"What would I have amounted to if I stayed here? Sure
Jesus I still haven't amounted to anything but at least I
gave it a try and tried to better myself. But you? What
the fuck did you ever do? You just sat here playing the
good country girl part to a tee. Kept your mouth shut and
just got on with it, you'd have sworn it was the 1950's!"
"I couldn't have coped. You know what this town is like.
Every single person would've known within 24 hours
and every one of them would have looked down on me.
They'd have judged me and shunned me, you were there,
and you remember what happened to Mary Moore. Even
the teachers in the school turned on her when she started
to show. I was doing ok in school, I couldn't afford to
ruin my life."
"Is that really what would have happened?"
"Of course it is! I couldn't have owned up to my
situation. I didn't tell anyone. Well except you and I
regret that to this day. For fuck's sake Derek, my Mam
shuffled on to her reward thinking I was this pure girl

who stayed at home with her to mind her by choice not because I felt so guilty about what I did. I told her I was happy to stay there and hold off having kids until I was ready. Who's ever ready? And look at me now; I'm 33 years of age, no husband, no kids, no boyfriend even. What if my only chance to have a child was when I was 17 and I CHOSE not to? You've no idea what is like to live with that guilt. Of course you don't 'cos you fucked off to the builders' yards at the first opportunity. You never even asked me what I was going to do, you just ran. I was so isolated, I was so alone and that shame eats away at me each and every day."

Charlie had got to her feet and was marching around the sitting room as she hammered home her points. But this last outburst took the last of her energies and she slouched on to the armchair. "I'm done" she finally whispered "I'm finished" as thoughts of playing with and caring for HER child flooded her mind; a child who'd be 17 by now.

"You're the only one who knows about my pregnancy and you've never once looked to support me. All you've done is use it to your advantage. You used it as an excuse to run away and you've used this secret as a stick to beat me with and take advantage of me; just exactly like you did when you were 16."

It was Derek's turn to take to his feet and assume control of the floor. "Now you listen to me and you listen to me good." Derek was jabbing a grubby finger in Charlie's direction, his voice a whisper but carrying the weight of real menace. "You don't be getting any ideas about yourself. I'm the one in charge of this situation right? I'll stay here as long as I want to. And you'll fucking well like it or believe me I'll stroll through this fucking backwater tomorrow morning telling everyone I can find about how Charlene, the local golden girl, was a teenage slapper who got herself in trouble and scurried away to Dublin and then to Chester to get an abortion. While all the while her sister and brother-in-law tried and tried in vain to start a family of their own. How do you think that'd go down with the locals? With your Mam worm-feed, yis are all that's left for each other, so imagine how alone you'd feel without them in your life?

So believe you me Charlie girl, you'll tell me every fucking detail about what's going on with Paul or I'll fucking finish you, you tramp. If you've gotten any ideas in your head about confiding in anyone they better leave your head just as sharpish."

Charlie had been reduced to a blubbering mess on the couch. All the strength she'd shown to move on with her life and do the best for herself was going to prove worthless. This animal, who she thought she had seen the last of forever, was back and could torpedo her at any second. She had learnt the hard way how manipulative Derek could be and she didn't think she had the strength to fight him off again.

Eventually she managed to compose herself and began to respond to Derek who was by now sitting smugly on the couch again. "Paul told me his story in confidence and I can't betray that. You know how private and structured that man is and I don't want to break his trust."

"But you're going to aren't you?" Derek sat back, crossed legs as a huge leer broke out across his face with the smug satisfaction of beating her again.

"It all started a long, long time ago in 1990 long before he and his wife moved here......." Charlie continued with as few accurate details as she could while her brain worked overtime trying to protect herself from Derek and protect herself from breaking Paul's confidence at the same time. "They were only recently married and having a bit of a tough time...." Just then she tailed off and thought to herself 'Fuck it, that might just work, even if it is my only option'.

27.

"There is also the recommendation that at the point of ejaculation the male can simply withdraw."
"Simply? Not for a million quid could I do that, not a chance!"
Maintaining some degree of order was becoming more and more difficult for Dr Hughes. He was trying his best but the futility of his efforts was beginning to show. It wasn't his fault he was here. He hated doing these school talks and year on year the kids knew more and were less shy about expressing their views.
"Well sonny, if that's going to be such a chore for you, you could always try abstinence. I know being good Catholic teenagers, attending a catholic secondary school that's your plan anyway isn't it?!" Dr Hughes was trying to inject a little humour into proceedings and show he was on their side and only wanted them to be careful but his heart wasn't in it and what was worse was that this group could sense that. So instead of a sarcastic tone, he delivered the line in a preachy, judgmental way. He could almost hear himself saying 'what would you know anyway?' Immediately the students responded the way they always did.
"Oh absolutely doctor, that's exactly what we're all going to do. Abstinence is the only way to continue the human race and sure aren't we all pioneers as well?" This comment brought cheers and applause from the assembled group. Dr Hughes wasn't a teacher so they didn't feel the need to even pretend they respected him. Then a voice spoke up from the back.

"Ahem, excuse me, Dr Hughes, Old McDonald here from the Farmers' Journal. You suggest that abstinence and being a pioneer are the way forward correct? Yet we sit here today in the company of two pregnant girls, most of us struggling with a hangover, listening to a sex-education talk in March of our final year in school. Your thoughts?"

Dr Hughes stood up from his desk at the top of the room and turned to face 'The Journalist'. "Far be it from me to speak on behalf of the 2 young ladies here today who are pregnant but I'd have to say there is only one possible explanation"

"Which is?"

"Well McDonald it's simple. It's all about the Immaculate Conception. Sure aren't we all good Catholics?!"

The gathered sixth year students burst in to hysterics. It couldn't have gone better if he had planned it. Dr Hughes let them have their moment before speaking again. Thinking all the time if you can't beat them, join them.

"You're absolutely right to laugh at the scenario here today kids. Well you're not kids are you? Here I am trying to explain the birds and the bees to 17/18 year olds while two of your fellow students sit here pregnant. I don't want to be here, you don't want to be here but it is part of the requirements of the system before you leave school so we've got to get on with it."

The students began to settle down a little and respected Dr Hughes for telling them the truth and saying it like it is. They may not have known it all but they knew a lot. They could probably teach the doctor a thing or two. So for everyone's sake he decided to get through the material as quickly as he could.

"This is great Doc, testify about the birds and the bees, but remember before you tell us the most important fact to come from the talk, there's something you have to do?"

"Really? And what is that son?"

"You withdraw from the room!"

****

"God bless him, he tried to keep it going but it wasn't going to work out was it?" The girls of St Malachys 6th year were giggling to themselves as they left the lecture hall. "Poor Dr Hughes hadn't a hope of getting anyone to concentrate on penises, fallopian tubes and STI's after Derek's comment about withdrawing."

The girls were in little groups of two's and three's looking over at Derek taking the high fives off his mates. They all looked at him in awe. While some of them might think of the odd smart comment they would never speak up but Derek didn't give a fuck who heard his jokes once they got a laugh. There was a rumour going around that he wasn't even going to sit his Leaving Certificate so he didn't care what the teachers tried to threaten him with.

Derek was still getting high fives off the football team and they blocked the door for ages. Charlene just wanted to get out of the room and away from all talk of sex and the rest. She did a good job of staring at the floor as she waited but just for a split-second she looked up and happened to catch Derek's eye. Just for a brief moment his façade slipped and his laughter faded. As she looked inside him Charlie could see the anger and the nastiness he felt for her. Underneath the classroom clown there was a vicious, manipulative bully. He was the only other person in the assembly who knew that quite easily Dr Hughes could've been speaking to a group with 3 pregnant girls not two.

Charlene eventually got out of the door and followed her friends to their chemistry class in silence. She had never felt so alone and isolated. Her friends were great people and they'd shared some amazing times growing up but right now Charlie was all alone even though she was surrounded by not only her friends but a teaching staff she liked and admired.

"You're gone very quiet Charlie? All that talk of dicks and sex and the rest a bit much for ya? Don't worry, even the good, quiet girls like yourself get to have sex but we just need to find you a nice fella who understands you and all you do for your mother and doesn't judge you for staying in with her at the weekends."

Charlie just smiled, smiled weakly and sat into her seat at the back of the chemistry lab. How could she tell them what she was going through? She couldn't. Where would she start in approaching the subject or talking to her teachers? She wouldn't. How could she get everyone past the judgement and the shame that the truth would bring on her? She couldn't.

Everything had to be a secret and it had to be kept that that way. Derek had slept with her, she hadn't asked him to wear a condom, and she had never spoken to her GP about the pill. She'd brought this on herself and anyway how could she talk to the GP about private stuff when he shared all the gossip after a few pints on Friday evenings. She could never have trusted him not to tell her mother's friends that she was taking the pill. And once they heard, they'd presume she was sleeping around with every young fella in the town.

Would anyone be able to understand that she couldn't have a baby at 17? How would the Priest who came to their house with communion for her mother react to news that she was pregnant? Or even worse, how would he react when he found out her only thought after Derek slept with her was to make sure a baby was never a possible outcome?

The Priest would stop coming to visit her mother at home and neither of them would be welcome in the church again. No matter what was happening and what she had to put herself through, she could never, ever, do that to her mother. Mary Hegarty had lived her tough life with only one constant throughout, The Catholic Church. She trusted, she lived and she loved her church and her faith. Charlie couldn't know for certain how her mother would react but she could never let her down that way. Telling her she wanted an abortion after falling victim to the basest instincts would destroy everything Mary believed in and the way she had lived her life for 60 years.

Chemistry was the last thing on Charlie's mind as the teacher entered the classroom. For more important were her future, her health, her sick mother and the judgement and scorn of rural Ireland. Rummaging through her schoolbag and realising she didn't have her chemistry homework with her wasn't exactly on that level.

28.

"You ready to go love?" Charlie's mam was worried she'd be late for school. Very rarely however did she ever get on to her about it. Charlie spent every spare second she had caring for her mother and this bought her some leeway with Mary. As Charlie breezed back into the sitting room her mother continued.

"Do you want me to sign your journal in case you're late again this morning?"

"Not at all mammy, if I needed one I could very easily copy your x but the teachers know what's going on and they give me time to make sure you're all sorted before I get into school."

"I'm so proud of you Charlene, you take great care of me and keep doing well in school, we'll have you off to college come September now too, you're a credit to yourself. But if you ever forge my signature, even if it is an x, I'll recover the use of my legs to chase you down!"

"You wouldn't mam, the first place you'd run is the hairdressers, we both know that!" Charlie bent down to kiss her mother goodbye. She loved to hear her mother laughing before she left for school, it reduced the worry she carried until she got home. "The school know I've to see you right and your tea and toast is there beside you, nice and cold, and Lily will be in at lunchtime to mind you because I've the debating meeting. I'll see you this evening though to get your dinner on and sort you out for bed ok?"

"Will I be on my own all day then Charlene? Until dinner?"

If Charlene's patience was wearing in any way thin, she disguised it brilliantly. She moved back to her mother and knelt down at her arm, saying in a patient tone, "you won't be alone mam, Lily will be in at lunchtime and I'll be well home after school before dinner time. I'll see you later mam, love you" Charlie kissed her mother's forehead and made for the hall door.

Slowly but surely her mother had been deteriorating, her short-term memory and concentration were worse than ever. Charlie knew she could do nothing else but look after her mother. Even when it meant she was late to school a couple of times, the teachers supported her because they knew she worked doubly hard to make up for any time she missed.

This was why she felt so terrible for lying to them all on top of her own internal guilt.

Her mother was Charlie's life really but she didn't need to know about how stupid she'd been. Mary wouldn't be able to comprehend it anyway so there was nothing to be gained from telling her. Her teachers were another story however. They'd given of their free time and energy to help. They'd stayed after school with her and they'd given her the support to carry on when it all got too much. And how had she repaid all that help?

She let Derek Flynn of all people get her pregnant. He'd slept with here and when there was no mention of a condom, she was naïve enough to believe it wouldn't happen to her. It was only the girls who slept around who got pregnant young. That was what she thought of the girls in her year so why would anyone think differently of her? She couldn't live with that shame.

Charlie knew she had only one option and that was why she'd deliberately left the house late this morning. She wanted to be sure everyone, students and teachers, were already in school before she appeared on Main Street. She couldn't risk being seen walking away from St Malachys and towards the city bus stop.

After putting her mother to bed last night, she'd done a little research. It wasn't like she could ask just anyone, 'so em, how do I go about terminating my pregnancy?' Nobody in her circles spoke about the possibility of getting an abortion to any great degree. And if they did it was only to say that it wasn't right for 'loose young women' to 'solve' their problems so 'quickly and easily' and with no difficulty over the decision.

As Charlie stepped on to the bus for Dublin, she wondered how her mother, her teachers, even her friends would react to the news. But that was all she could do because she'd never be able to take the chance of telling anyone the truth. She'd been forced to keep everything secret from the people she trusted and valued the most. She may have been able to convince them this was the right decision for her to take but she could never take that risk. Besides she saw how Tina and Suzanne had been treated by the school.

Nothing was ever said to the girls directly but it had been made obvious that they'd washed their hands of them. According to them the girls had ruined their lives and the teachers weren't going to waste time on girls who didn't listen to the preaching. No it was much better to invest time in kids like Charlene Hegarty. The kind of good girl, who listened, learned and was too respectful, both of others and themselves, to get in to trouble.

Charlie had seen this happening and although it'd never been said in so many words, she had felt that vibe from the teachers who did extra work with her. And then she had gone and let herself be caught out. How could she be relied upon to be a parent and a guide for a young child in her situation?

'For fuck's sake I'm a child myself. I'm terrified of all the judgement that will come down on me and I've been forced into making this decision by myself because I put myself out there as one of the good girls. No matter how difficult or painful this is going to be you've got to do it Charlie and you've got to do it alone.'

The bus pulled out of Kilcastle and Charlie stared at her reflection in the glass. She was alone and isolated. She would have to deal with the shame and destruction on her own and then live with it for the rest of her life. But she was so confused by the attitudes she encountered around her. In so many ways she felt like she was making a responsible, considered and correct decision for herself. But would anyone else think that way or would they be swayed to thinking that what she was doing was shameful, disgusting, foolish and helpless? Terminating her pregnancy was a massive consideration but being forced to keep it secret, in spite of the fact it felt right to her, left Charlie completely lost and bewildered. Charlie bundled her coat between her head and the glass and sobbed and cried all the way to Dublin. This was going to be a momentous day, for better or for worse hadn't been decided yet.

29.

"Do you want to come over and we can sort out the guest list for the New Year's Eve party?"
"I don't know Charlie; I'm not even sure about having a party in your gaff for New Year. And anyway your mam never liked me being in your house when were just in school together. What'll she say if I suddenly appear over this afternoon on my own?"
"Well you don't have to worry about that today. Mam's over with Sharon today so it'll just be the two of us."
"Ah you should've started with that bit of information. Right I'll be over in ten minutes so."
Derek didn't wait for any sort of reply before hanging up on Charlie. He ran upstairs to check his hair in the mirror and spray some of his potent scent. He was talking to himself as he locked up his house.
'This'll be fun! Charlie has the house to herself for the afternoon and wants me to come over? Today must be going to be the day so. It couldn't be anything else. For fucks sake man you've put in the effort and been very patient with her. She's wanted it all along but she's decided at last that she's going to get it today.'
Halfway to Charlie's house, Derek checked his sprint and settled into a fast walk. There were very few things that he could do very well and he knew he was on the interesting side of good looking. But something about the cockiness and the little bit of jack the lad in him appealed to the local girls of the town. They liked to pretend they didn't feel that way but they all wanted to be treated the way he treated them. He never questioned

it too much; in fact he enjoyed the reputation as one of the heartbreakers of the town. And lo and behold here was goody two shoes herself falling for his, inexplicable, charms. He ran over and over in his mind the fun he'd have with Charlene, and if she relaxed and let herself, she might even enjoy it too.

Once Derek had hung up on her, Charlie made for the kitchen to get ready for his arrival. She didn't think he'd be so enthusiastic about organising the party. But if she could host a good party and unveil Derek as her fella at the same time, well then everyone would remember where they were that New Year's Eve.

She picked up her notebook and post-it notes from the table. Charlie was wondering about everything she'd heard about Derek in school. They'd had a kiss at Helen's party a few weeks back but that was all that started things. Derek hadn't looked for any more that night and then he'd taken nearly a week to speak to her outside of school because, as he said himself, he was too shy to make his feelings obvious in school.

Charlie had seen no sign of the Derek his exes had told her about. He wasn't very possessive and while her Mam didn't really like him, he'd been respectful around her and always walked her home to the door. But apart from getting a bit handsy now and again he'd been a decent guy. So Charlie had begun to wonder if maybe all the stories she'd heard about him being a prick and sleeping around were just the bitter comments of scorned ex-girlfriends.

As soon as Derek rang the bell, Charlie had the hall door open. She was excited about the party and what the next few weeks would bring that she'd watched the garden path until he'd arrived. 'He hasn't kissed me like this before' she thought as his hand slipped down her back before cradling an ass cheek. She held him close, enjoying the tingle she felt as they kissed. His hands were moving all over her back and only stopped when he felt the thick bra strap through her shirt. 'That's disappointing but it won't slow me down too much' he thought and carried on kissing her.

"Come on let's get started!" Charlie said as she turned and took his hand to lead the way. "My thoughts exactly!" Derek enthused, looking forward to sleeping with Charlene for the first time. So needless to say he was shocked when, still holding his hand, Charlene led him past the stairs and towards the kitchen.

"Now I've started making a few lists for the party. There are all my friends on one, anyone you want to invite on another, the food we'll need to get and do we need to buy any drink for here? Or will we just tell people to bring their own?" Charlie was in full flow, firing question after question in Derek's direction; while he was stuck in the door jamb of the kitchen. The look of pure confusion on his face betraying him, this wasn't the way it was supposed to be.

Charlie looked up for a split-second and noticed his puzzlement. "I know it's amazing isn't it all the things you need to think about to organize the party. So much for just getting Mam to Sharon's and having a party. We need to sort out all the other stuff. This'll be the first time with us properly together and I want it to go perfectly. Will you come in out of the doorway and sit down?"

Derek eventually joined Charlie at the kitchen table. Disappointed as he was that they weren't taking full advantage of the free house, Derek consoled himself that there was a long afternoon ahead of them. Plus if he listened attentively and helped Charlie with the planning, well it'd be rude of her not to repay his kindness then. Charlie continued, blissfully unaware of the especially lusty urges rushing through Derek's body. "I've listed out my friends that I'm going to invite. Who are you going to invite? Just so I can have an idea of numbers." "Bloody hell Charlie, I hadn't thought of inviting anyone. I mean it's a party, I just presumed we'd say it in school and then whoever turns up, turns up." "The problem with that though Derek is the lads from the bottom class. If they get whiff of a party they'll ruin this house or the lads from the Grange estate, remember what they did to Aideen's house at Halloween?" "Easy on Charlie, remember I live beside that estate and I've grown up playing ball with most of those lads. And anyway it wasn't that bad in Aideen's was it? Just a few spills and shit like that." "Well those spills and shit added up to about €800 and I can't afford something like to happen and mam definitely can't." "Ok, ok I won't say it to any of those lads, I'll leave you do the inviting and sure I can keep an eye on the front door on the night for you." What a shout Derek thought to himself, that sort of chivalry will have to be rewarded. Even with the long list of everything that Charlie wanted to go through, the planning only took about a half hour. Bring your own beer, pick up the balloons and get Derek to put his CD collection together. Charlie's taste in music wouldn't stand up to many cool tests. Her party wasn't going to be remembered for her poor taste in music anyway.

"Perfect, that's everything sorted I think, you want a cup of tea?"

Derek was up off his chair and after Charlie before she reached the kettle. "I might have a cuppa but not yet babe, I have a much better way to pass the time." He spun Charlie around to face him and with his hands around her shoulders he pulled her close. Enjoying the feel of her breasts against his chest he lunged in to kiss her. His kiss was urgent, full of tongue and expectation. This was finally going to happen. She was finally going to let him in and he was finally going to be able to caress her tight, naked body. "Come on babe, that was a good idea to get me over here for the party but we know the real reason I'm here. It's time."

Charlie stopped kissing him and tried to push him away with her hands. "Whoa, whoa, I DID only ask you over to help arrange the party. Oh my God, you thought we were gonna…..? I mean you know I'm not ready, I've told you how I want my first time to be special, I've told you I'm not and that's definitely not what today's about."

"Don't be such a fuckin' tease Charlie you know you want this, especially after sending your Mam away to Sharon's house." Derek was too strong for Charlie to push away; instead he moved his hands to her ass and pulled her close. So close in fact that there was no doubting Derek's readiness.

"I'm not doing this today Derek, it's not gonna happen. It's not the way I'm losing my virginity. I know you want to and you've done it before so it's not a big deal. But I haven't and it's a big deal to me."

"You're a fuckin' whore!" Derek exploded. "You string me along, make a point of inviting me over when you're alone and you still won't fuck me?"

"I invited you over when Mam was out 'cos she isn't sure about you but I am. Well at least I was. I don't like this side of you Derek, I think you should go."

"Me hole am I walking out that door now! I know you want it and you know what as well? It'll feel great and then we'll be closer than ever."

Derek grabbed Charlie's hand and began to drag her towards the hall and the stairs. "No Derek, no, get off me, not like this, I'm not ready, let me go!" Charlie was trying desperately to stop and pull away back towards the kitchen but between his strength and her socks slipping on the wooden floor, she couldn't. She flailed her arms and legs with all she had but Derek was too strong and slowly and terrifyingly it began to dawn on Charlie what Derek was capable of and what was about to happen.

Just five minutes later Derek was re-buckling his belt as he pulled the Hegarty's hall door closed. "You made me do this Charlie, you brought it on yourself with the teasing and what's more I know it's what you really wanted too." With that Derek stopped speaking over his shoulder and slammed the front door behind him, leaving just the awful sound of silence behind.

The silence was punctured by Charlie's wracking sobs. She curled herself into the foetal position at the bottom of the stairs. She had fought with everything but she realised that no matter how hard she fought Derek wouldn't stop until he got what he wanted. She decided the whole ordeal would be over quicker if she didn't fight as much. And so it had been.

Derek was spent in no time at all after taking her there on the stairs. It had been the complete opposite of how Charlie had imagined her first time to be. Lying at the bottom of the stairs Charlie felt so used and dirty. She was in huge physical pain but she also felt guilty and ashamed. Guilty about what she'd made Derek do, maybe she HAD led him on? Maybe it wasn't fair to ask for patience of a teenage boy?

Guilty, ashamed, dirty and broken. This was only the beginning.

30.

Charlie was back on the bus and heading for home in next to no time. Walking up to the clinics door, she had noted that everybody on the street was looking at her, everybody was watching her and commenting on her activities and worst of all every word was being relayed to her ailing mother lying in bed at home.

Knowing not a sinner in Dublin was a good thing. That was why Charlie travelled to Dublin to visit the clinic. 'Imagine having to ask her Dr Hughes at home for the morning after pill? Jesus I'd never live it down and he'd be telling everyone' she thought 'and by that of course he'll tell Mam at a moment's notice. He'd say he was looking out for me but he loves being the guardian and then the spreader of all secrets and news and he'd love to drop me in it.'

'No I'm right; Dublin is the best place for me to go. But why am I so scared?' Charlie lived just 25 miles from Dublin's O'Connell Street but she never ventured in. Everything she could ever need was available much more locally. So while it was true she knew no one in Dublin but by the same token, she didn't know anyone in Dublin who could help her.

She wasn't sure of where to go when she arrived into Dublin. Directions weren't easy to come by, and it wasn't like she could just go up to anyone and ask them was it? As soon as she mentioned Irish Family Planning Association whoever she asked would be judging her, looking her up and down and wondering how she'd come to be 'fallen'.

As she walked into the fourth shop she'd been in since Busaras Charlie finally caught sight of someone working who was under 30 years old. Eventually she gathered what little confidence she had and sidled up to a youngish man who didn't look like he'd judge her. Charlie was a good girl who'd never taken drugs but she imagined even drug deals were conducted in louder whispers then she used to speak to him.

Very slowly, gently he told her where she was to go and even made her repeat the directions back so he was sure she knew where she was going. Now as she followed the route she noticed how many churches she was passing on the way. 'We're going to let you get the pill Charlie, but, as a country, we're going to make you walk past church after church. This way you'll have plenty of opportunity to think about what you're doing and come to the correct decision. We're going to make you think of all the people you're letting down. We're here to remind you that if you get rid of that baby that may be in your womb now; you won't be welcome in our places of worship again. We won't let you look your mother in the eye while she receives communion, unaware of your sin. You're a disgrace.'

Nobody needed to say a word to Charlie, she heard everybody passing her saying similar words. She spotted the clinic door from a long way off and then felt terrified because it was overlooked on nearly every side by offices, shops and restaurants. She walked around at a distance watching to see if anyone else went in or out of the door. Nobody did. All she could do was imagine how, as soon as she put her hand on it, the door would set off an alarm and everyone on the street would turn and abuse her. Up until 24 hours ago, Charlie had never ever thought about this scenario but without any chat, all these thoughts were engrained on her psyche and became her natural response to her situation.

Eventually she gently approached the door, praying, yes that's ironic she thought, that no alarms would go off, she could slip in unnoticed and the doctor wouldn't be too judgemental. This finally brought a brief smile to her face for the first time in ages. There she was going in to get the pill or whatever she needed not to be pregnant, praying to God the doctor would be nice, while knowing society and catholic Ireland would disown her for that very action. 'This is some fucked up country I live in' she whispered to herself and then apologised to God for the profanity. 'Can I ever win God?' she thought and pushed the door in to the clinic.

****

"Is your Mam feeling any better today then Charlene?" All of her teachers had taken her to their hearts. She was a very beautiful and also a very quiet and studious teenager. Yet there was so much more to her than that. Her father had never been around for her, having left before she was born. Her older sister resented her arrival on the scene and so Charlie's Mam became everything to her. She was both parents, a mentor, a guide but also a friend and someone who attempted to be her sibling too. "It must be tough on you both at the minute Charlene? Between you trying to prepare for the Leaving Cert. and the care your mother needs? That was why you missed yesterday I presume?" Mrs. Raftery, her English teacher, was always a step above the other teachers for Charlie. "Yeah that's exactly it Miss, she had a rough weekend with the pain and neither of us was able to get much sleep. So I just couldn't face lessons yesterday on top of that. I'm sorry again Miss." Charlie lied. She hated lying, especially to people who gave her so much. But she couldn't risk telling them the truth. They were still her teachers. They were still from a different generation. They could never understand and they would judge her so much. They would definitely change their attitudes towards her. No, she had decided, they could never know the truth. "Yeah I stayed with her and caught up with some sleep as she slept."

"That's ok Charlie, we can manage that and get by. But you've got to let us know you won't be in. One of us could drop work out to you and have a cuppa with you. We want to help you and you don't have to go through this alone."

'Oh but I do!' thought Charlie, the guilt of lying to these people was building up inside her. The shame at how stupid she'd been to think Derek could change and ashamed at how much she'd let them all down. How she had lied to them and how she had taken advantage of the trust they had in her. The tears built in her eyes as she thought about the whole situation, this massive mess she found herself in. "Thanks Miss, I hope you know how much I appreciate your support and the things you do for me?" Charlie managed to get the words out of her mouth between sobs and the power behind this further lie, forced more tears from her eyes.

Mrs. Raftery held her close and whispered in her ear that everything would be alright and that Charlie would get through the hard times with her mother. 'You can tell her Charlie, you can tell this lady the truth. She would understand and she would support you. She might even be able to help you.' But just as quickly as these thoughts shot into her mind they were assailed by more negative thoughts. 'Don't tell her a fucking thing. You can't tell anybody, you've made your decision and now you've got to stick to it. You can't predict how anyone in this church ruled country is going to react. Why else do women have to leave for an abortion or go to Dublin for the morning after pill? They say it's illegal, it's immoral and they'll throw you to the fires of hell for eternity!' Charlie was completely confused and unsure of what or who to believe in. She continued to cry into Mrs. Raftery's arms but it wasn't about her mother, it was about herself. From somewhere deep inside her she heard that timid, frightened voice inside her whisper again, 'but it's the right thing for me to do, why can't everyone see that?'

31.

"Charlene Hegarty get over here this instant!" Mrs.
Raftery had pulled sentry duty for the arrival of the St.
Malachys students. School ties, correctly tightened, and
correct shoes, well-polished, weren't on her radar today.
Not even the 'Orange Ladies' covered in make-up or the
rebels with their piercings on show. She had only one
face in her sights today and that was Charlie Hegarty.
"What did I tell you, just the other week, about telling
me the truth when you have to miss school to mind your
mother? Don't you remember me saying that we'd find a
way around it? But that could only happen if you rang
and let us know the full story. Why weren't you in
school on Friday?"
"I had to mind my Mam; she wasn't in a very good
way." Charlie's answer barely reached Mrs. Raftery's
ears as it was directed squarely at the floor. She was
afraid to meet her teachers' eye.
"Please Charlie; please don't make it worse by lying to
me. I drove out to your house at lunchtime with some
notes for you and there was no sign of you."
"It must have been when I went to the chemists, we must
have just missed each other......."
"Charlie? Stop please, just stop lying. I know you
weren't there. I was speaking to your mother's home-
helper and even through her broken English, she was
adamant you had left very early to go to school. And this
got me to thinking, why would Charlie lie to me? Is she
gone on the hop? Has my good nature been taken
advantage of? Have you been laughing at me behind my

back every time I put myself out to help you? Do you ever NEED to stay at home with your mother at all? Or have you just been taking a day off whenever you wanted and blaming it on your mother?"

"No Miss I'd never do anything like that, my mam does need a lot of help, so some days she needs me to help her out as well as the home-help. But I just went off on the hop for the day. I couldn't face up to the pressure and the stress of everything, I just needed a break." The lies came so easily for Charlie nowadays, practice was making perfect. "I probably should have told you or come to you first but I swear that's the only time I've done it."

"But you see Charlie, I just can't be certain that's the truth. I've seen every situation being exploited by teenagers in school to suit themselves. I definitely felt you were different and maybe I'm too cynical but I can't be sure. We've given you a lot of leeway this year and I've gone out on a limb personally to protect you when other teachers wanted to throw you on the academic scrapheap. You usually call me aside when you're struggling with the expectations on you so why was this time different? Have you been playing me all along or what was so different this time that you couldn't come to me?"

"No of course I haven't Miss. There's nothing at all going on that's different. The Leaving Cert. is close now and I'm beginning to worry about them on top of minding Mam."

"But you've always excelled in exams and you're not the type to get nervous, in spite of all your timidity. If you don't want to talk to me that's up to you but I'm going to be checking on every day you're absent from now until the end of the year. It might be that you're just taking advantage of the freedom we give you but I don't think that's like you at all. If it is then I'll be disappointed for you but also for myself because I thought I could read teenagers quite well after all my years of teaching."

****

The day the Leaving Certificate results are released is an odd day for teachers and students alike. Another group of young adults will leave school behind them and move on to the next stage of their lives. The choices they made over which subjects to study and how hard to work, all have the potential to impact on the rest of their lives. The pressure to achieve is enormous but three months after they put down their pens, the stress about results is present but there is absolutely nothing they can do about how they performed.

For the teachers of St. Malachys comprehensive, watching the young men and women collect their results in their 'civvies' was as good a time as any to take stock of their achievements. Individual teachers wanted their students to have got the result they deserved as their final grade. But as a group, they surveyed the assembled young adults and wondered how they had done in preparing them for the outside world.

Mr. Burrell, the maths teacher, liked to be strict with his students, hoping to motivate them through a fear of failure. Mrs. Raftery, meanwhile, tried to see the talent in everyone and wanted to see them excel in that area, even if that wasn't English and was being a caring and mature person. No exam could measure that but all the teachers, and all their different ways of teaching, had moulded these 17/18 year olds into the people before them. Not everyone could achieve academic success but as Mrs. Raftery would repeat in the staff room, "I think we've enabled them all to maximise their potential, whatever that may be for each one of them." Some students were over the moon simply to pass every exam. Some were disappointed not to get the grades required for their number one college choice despite relatively impressive marks. But as they collected their grades, in ones, twos and threes, there weren't any major surprises in the teachers' eyes. Then Charlie Hegarty walked in.

She collected her envelope from the principal with barely a grunt and turned to walk straight back out the front door. She didn't speak to anyone, she didn't look at anyone. She had dark rings under both eyes and she walked completely hunched over like someone carrying the weight of the world on their shoulders.

Mrs. Raftery had called to her house twice since the end of the school year. But both times she had received short shrift. Charlie had become extremely isolated and withdrawn in the last two months of school, in fact almost from the moment she had confronted Charlie about missing school. Charlie barely spoke to her after that incident which was in stark contrast to the times earlier in the year when she would stop by her office just for a cup of tea and a chat. She used these times as a distraction from her studies and being the primary carer for her mother. Mrs. Raftery continued to feel guilty about driving a wedge between them but Charlie never opened her mouth about it.

In fact, Charlie never said a word to anyone about anything these days. She had stopped meeting up with her school friends, blaming the studying before the exams and having to mind her mother since them. Somehow in spite of everything, Charlie had managed to secure an impressive set of results and Mrs. Raftery wanted to acknowledge that.

"Well done Charlene, you did brilliantly!" she said crossing the canteen, her arms outstretched to give her a hug. "How are you feeling? You must be delighted? How have you been? Are you very tired?"

Charlie didn't reciprocate the hug and waited for the grip to be released. "Yeah I'm fine" was all she said. Mrs. Raftery looked at her quizzically, trying to figure out which question that was the answer to.

"Well you'll be starting college soon though, yeah? I mean, with those points you'll get your first choice in Trinity won't you?" Mrs Raftery was delighted for Charlie and what she had come through to attend her alma mater. Charlie had a pin for her celebration balloon though.

"It doesn't matter what they offer me or even what college it is. I'm not going."

"What do you mean not going? Sure the offers haven't come out yet but you're a shoe-in."

"It doesn't matter woman will you listen to me. My Mam needs me to look after her. I can't leave her to go off to college with money we don't have."

"But there are grants Charlie, supports for you and your mam, there's….."

"For fuck's sake you're not listening to me. It didn't matter what results I got, it doesn't matter what I'm offered, if anything, all that matters is my mam. I've got to be there for her and I won't leave her alone. Listen I've got to go, ok?"

Charlie turned on her heel and made for the door, leaving Mrs. Raftery more confused than ever, with her mouth agape. Where was the caring, bright young lady of four months earlier gone? How had she misread a student, something she prided herself on, so badly? It made no sense. She still hadn't moved when Charlie reached the door and turned to see her teacher one last time. "Miss?" she called back into the canteen. Mrs. Raftery looked at her, her eyes soft with tears of sadness.

'Thank you for everything' Charlie mouthed while wiping tears from her own eyes with her cuffs. A smile played on Mrs. Raftery's face for a split second as Charlie voiced her gratitude. Ultimately it confused her more however. Where had she gone wrong with this vulnerable girl? In spite of it all, had she been of any real help? Mrs. Raftery would never see Charlie again to ask her but she made herself believe that had to be the case.

32.

"So what time do we have to be ready to leave at in the morning Lou?" Louise was so taken aback by her Dad's question that she temporarily lost the ability to speak. She had barely got herself over the threshold of the house after her visit to the hairdressers and felt blindsided.

"Bloody hell Da, I'm barely in the door"

"I know love but it jumped in to my head when I saw you and you know me I'd have forgotten to ask if I waited until later."

Louise wasn't just taken aback by the timing of Paul's question but by the fact he was even aware of her graduation at all. He was always there for Jack and her but at the same time he was never really there. They always spoke to Maura about their lives and what they were up to. Maura then passed on the information to Paul whenever she needed to. They all lived in the same house but they had very little direct interaction.

"I just presumed you'd just turn up when Mam told you, if you were coming at all. Thanks for the money for my hair by the way."

"No problem love, I thought you might want to look your best on your big day."

"I do look good don't I Mam?" Louise asked turning away from her father.

"You do love, that Aisling is an artist. Not that you don't always look good anyway but you know what I mean. I'm just digging a hole for myself." Maura decided to change the subject. "I suppose if we get a taxi about 12ish that'll give us plenty of time won't it?"

"Yeah definitely Mam, like I just need to be there before everyone else to practice my speech ya know?"

"You're making a speech?" Paul interjected "when did that come about?"

"Jesus Dad! You can zone out so much at times! Did Mam not tell you?" Louise decided to continue as if talking to a child. "Right, so you know in a school there's girls from about 12-18 yeah? And you know it can be a scary place for some 12 year olds? So some of the older girls take on the responsibility to look after them and they are called Prefects. I'm one of those girls, that's why I wear the badge on my uniform? Anyway I'm a special type of Prefect and my class asked the teachers if I could be the Head Girl. And when you're the Head Girl you get to make a speech at the graduation to wish all the girls well after they leave school. So that's why I'm making a speech tomorrow night!"

"Alright, alright smartarse, I must've just forgotten or something. You know how I am so old and all?" Paul decided to match Louise's sarcasm with some of his own.

"But God Dad if you just talked to me once in a while you'd have known that for certain!"

Paul bit his tongue. He'd gain nothing by biting her head off for that and he was trying to build a relationship with his daughter not destroy it completely. "Yeah you're right love I suppose but I'll be there tomorrow. It'll be nice to take a look around the school and even though I didn't know about it, I'll be very proud to listen to you speak tomorrow." Paul pushed himself to his feet decisively and moved towards Louise and the open door behind her. "Right you two probably want to talk about hair and make-up and nails so I'll make my exit stage left." Paul placed his hand on Louise's shoulder as he passed her. He didn't look at her really or say anything but Louise felt something comforting in his gesture. But all she could do was stare, open-mouthed, at her mother. She was responding with a mirror image facial expression. While the two Forsyth women stood in this still life tableau the front door slammed and Paul was off down The Local again.

****

353 Harbour Close was a hive of activity. Scents, aromas and hairspray swirled through the house as Maura and Louise readied themselves. Louise emerged from the bathroom, which looked more like a hotel steam room, and flounced past Paul on the landing. The steam followed her and Paul rubbed his eyes just to make sure his house did actually resemble a 1980's music video. Not only did the steam move in a cloud like a dry-ice and wind-machine, it was laced with the perfume of a particularly pungent shower cream Louise reserved for special occasions. It assaulted his hung-over nostrils and threatened him with vomiting like a teenager experimenting with the drink.
Making sure to breathe in as little as possible; Paul crossed the landing and made for the kitchen. Only a mug of his own strong coffee could help him back to life this morning. He hadn't planned a session last night but

knowing the day he had ahead of him today, he had reasoned a little Dutch courage wouldn't go amiss. Maura was putting on her makeup in the kitchen having showered early so as not to upset Louise and her preening plans.

"And where were you until closing time last night?" Maura asked without looking away from the mirror.

"Ah it was a quiet night down below so Andy asked me to hang on with him while he locked up." Paul lied. It came so easily to him and he never missed a beat as he filled the coffee machine.

"Go away out of that will you! Some poor sod put temptation in your way and you couldn't say no more likely"

"I swear, being a Tuesday there were only a few about and Andy was worried about being alone locking up. Anyway, will I be able to use MY bathroom at any stage or will Barbie need it again?"

"Don't be calling her that just because she cares how she looks. Just take your coffee and go shower…. And have a shave…….. And put on your blue shirt and tie……… And hurry up, the taxi is due in 20 minutes."

"I'll be ready woman" Paul whispered to himself "it's a big day for Louise but it is gonna be a big day for us too."

Eighteen and a half minutes later Paul ran down the stairs and pulled the door behind them, strips of toilet paper flying from his face where he'd put them after cutting himself shaving. He didn't bother putting on the alarm with Jack still in bed.

"You're early mate so you better not have started the meter trying to do me out of a few quid." Paul said as he made to get in the passenger seat. "Ah shite" he added as he ran back through the garden and in the front door. Maura and Louise looked quizzically at each other in the back of the car and apologised to the taxi driver as Paul re-emerged patting the front pocket of his suit jacket and slamming the hall door once again.

"Right let's go." Paul said pulling on his seatbelt. "How are you feeling about your speech Lou? Are you nervous or are you ready to go?"

"I'm grand now, it's not like the Leaving Certificate, you know, there's no wrong answer. I feel much better having practiced last night for Mam."

"Great stuff" said Paul ignoring the barb at his absence last night, "Malachys School please chief."

****

Sitting on an uncomfortable chair in the school hall Paul was dragged back to memories of his own school days. The Christian Brothers had beaten him through until his 16th birthday when he walked out the door without ever looking back. This focus on the physicality and violence of his own secondary school days jarred with the scenes he saw in St Malachys hall. Here and there teachers and students, male and female, shook hands with each other and exchanged hugs. The young men and women leaving the school had the utmost respect for their teachers but at the same time they felt comfortable and relaxed in their company.

Paul caught a glimpse of Louise backstage reading her notes. The Principal, or who Paul presumed was the Principal, wandered over towards her and must have asked how she was feeling because she let out a nervous looking giggle before composing herself again. She walked across the stage shaking hands or hugging at least four teachers. Paul could again only assume they were teachers because he'd never once met any of them. Jack and Louise had gone through 14 years of school each and Paul had never been to one parent-teacher meeting. A jealousy rose in him as he watched his daughter, a beautiful, quietly confident young woman and the easy rapport she enjoyed with her teachers and classmates. He'd never felt so out of step with his daughters life. These people had moulded her into who she was today. But Paul just felt jealous. Jealous of the rapport and the time they had spent together; jealous and a little nauseous again.

Maura reached for his hand as she turned away from the O'Moores and ushered him towards their seats. But Paul stopped, turned and patted his wife on her shoulder. "You've done a great job raising our children. They've been lucky to have you as their mother and their father." Paul turned away and excused himself as he passed another couple and sat in to the seats with their names on them. Maura was given no chance to reply or comment on Paul's massive declaration. She had barely been able to squeeze into the chair beside him before Principal Byrne moved to the small lectern on the stage. Following a long-winded welcome speech Principal Byrne began presenting certificates to each graduating student. All the parents had been told to wait until afterwards to take their photographs but when the first two sets of parents stood up and took pictures without being censored everybody decided to follow suit. As a result every student's name was accompanied by a round of applause, a flash of a smart phone and the screeching of chairs as parents moved all around trying to get to the best camera spots.

"Paul? Paul what are we going to do? I'm after forgetting the camera in the house. I left the battery on to charge and forget to take it with me. Will we ring Jack? Or will I ask someone else to take a picture for us? Oh God she'll be mortified if she's the only one up there not getting her photograph taken."

While his wife fretted, Paul was fiddling with his suit jacket and rustling papers like he was opening a sweet in the cinema. "What are you doing Paul? Are you listening to me at all? I'm after forgetting the camera."

Eventually Paul turned towards Maura and rather than give out he just smiled. He stopped fidgeting and brought a box-like object towards her lap. "I thought I might want or need this today so I stopped into the chemists on the way to the pub last night."

Excusing himself as he slipped passed the other people in his row; Paul made his way to the centre aisle of the school hall. He made it to the front of the stage just in time for Louise to walk along the stage towards Mr. Byrne. "Smile Louise!" he said as he brought the disposable camera up to eye level. "Wait, wait, I've to wind it on so I can take another one!" Louise was on diplomatic mode and luckily for Paul kept smiling just long enough for another picture. But just as Paul turned to go back to his seat, she shot him a look of disgust. He could tell she was embarrassed and she'd be having words with him about his archaic photography equipment. At the same time though, Paul felt a little oblivious to her looks. He was merely proud to have been there to capture the moment his daughter was leaving school.

"Principal Byrne, vice-Principal McGee, teachers, students, parents and everybody welcome to the graduation ceremony of St. Malachys comprehensive Class of 2014. I've been nominated to speak to you on behalf........."

Paul had continued smiling as he saw the gestures and heard the smart comments about the camera being as old as him and slipped back into his seat as Louise began her speech. Maura shot him a look she had taught her daughter as he sat down but out of Louise's view she squeezed Paul's hand and whispered. "That was such a nice thing to do Paul. You still have the ability to surprise me, even if Louise will never forgive you!" Maura made to move her hand away from Paul but he held it tight on his lap. They sat like that giving their full attention and beaming with pride at their daughter's accomplishments. 'Thanks for reminding me to pick up a camera James' Paul thought to himself.

33.

"Well done Louise, you made a beautiful speech and covered so many topics I think you must have included every student. I'm really, really proud of you."

"Thanks Mam, I'm just glad Ms. Ramsden spent plenty of time helping me out. I was really nervous too 'cos I don't even know some of the students in the bottom classes but she had helped me to mention a few things that were relevant to them."

"Well you did that and everybody was applauding when you finished!" Maura added.

"Well done Louise with the speech and the best of luck next year."

"Ah thanks very much, just have to get through the Leaving now!" Louise responded as the couple kept walking.

"Who are they Louise?" Maura asked

"No idea Mam to be honest but they seem to know me don't they? Here, what was Dad like with that disposable camera? God I was mortified, with everyone else using the smartphones and digital cameras."

Maura spotted Paul coming back from the toilet but didn't change her reply to Louise. "I know, I know love, it was a bit cringy but in all fairness to him it got us out of a tight spot. I forgot to take the camera battery out of the charger."

"You muppet ya Mam, God it was awful though with everyone else going before me, that just drew more attention to it." Louise hadn't realised her Dad was standing behind her and continued "everyone thought he was my Granddad first and then to see him holding up the ceremony winding on the fucking camera! I mean who winds on a camera now?"

"At least we got a photograph to remember the moment at all Lou, since your Mam forgot the digital one." Paul cut in trying desperately to hide the disappointment in his voice.

"I know Dad, I'm sorry; it was just such a surprise to see you with THAT camera."

"I probably embarrassed you Louise but I couldn't miss out on remembering a special moment in your life."

"Thanks Dad, I really do appreciate it but that thing is a relic. I mean we have to wait until you finish the feckin' roll before we can see the photo you took! What if you only took my feet or something?"

"We'll just have to finish the roll quickly so!" Paul said with genuine enthusiasm. Come on and we'll head down the Italian for a bite to eat. Jack said he'd meet us down there."

Louise and Maura led the way out of the school saying goodbye and taking the well wishes as they passed. They held the door open and Paul followed while saying "your speech was fantastic by the way Louise. You're a wonderful public speaker and it went down really well."

****

"That was a nice meal, thanks Dad. Food wasn't as good as yours Mam but it did the job!" Jack was in full wind up mood as they left Schillaci's.

"Easy on son. Did you enjoy it Louise? After all it is your day."

"Yes Dad it was lovely, thanks a million."
"Good stuff, what's the plan for later? Are you hitting the town with the gang tonight?"
"I haven't decided yet to be honest. I'm not really into paying over the odds to get drunk but I might drop in for a while ya know?"
Louise's answer hung in the air between the Forsyth's. They spent such little time together as a family conversation was never really in full flow. Nobody could really think of anything to add. So they strolled in silence for about 200 yards in the general direction of home when Paul stopped and turned back to his family.
"Right it's decision time. I'm heading to The Local for a pint. What are the rest of you doing?"
Maura looked around for an invite but after so many years she should have known better. So she simply said "I think I'll go home and get these shoes off and relax in front of the television."
"I'm heading to Dean's to play the computer." Jack said and Louise added that she'd probably head home and see about heading back out later in the evening.
"So nothing important then no?"
"No nothing at all Dad, same shit different shovel!" replied Jack on behalf of his mother and sister.
"Right well if that's the case so you may as well come with me for a drink. I think we could all do with a pint to celebrate Louise's day."
"Fuck off Dad and stop missing will you! The Local is a no-go area for the family, we all know that" Jack added. "I know you let me in from time-to-time but you really want to bring the women into your pub? Well I'm not going to miss that!"

Maura was too shocked to speak momentarily but finally managed to get a reply out, "I'd love to Paul but will I not be out of place? Will there be any other women in there tonight?"

"What about you Louise? It won't be much of a celebration without the guest of honour."

Louise wanted to go but she was also a little wary and unsure. "It's a great idea Dad, but why now? Why tonight?"

"I just wanted to spend some time with you all that's it" Paul lied.

"Jaysus Dad's on the way out and he's decided this is the moment to tell us!" Jack was genuinely worried about his Dad but felt slagging him and joking was his best form of protection.

"I'm not dying gobshite but I'll die of fucking thirst if we stand around here much longer. So come on, let's get going and get a drink in front of us." And with that the Forsyth's were off on a family outing to The Local, something none of them ever thought would be a possibility.

****

"Jesus Christ Paul, what are you doing here on a Wednesday night?"

"Just fancied a change of scene you know yourself. I had to get out of the house for a while, not a fan of them soaps!"

"I see" Charlie replied "I'd say the family are only glad to get rid of you for a few hours too. I'll start you up a roaster while you get settled."

200

Charlene was so busy slagging Paul, she hadn't really noticed the other 3 customers who had sheepishly made their way in the door behind him. They followed Paul up towards the top of the pub and settled themselves in to a low table under the side window. Paul meanwhile hung his coat up and approached his normal stool but didn't clamber up and stayed standing.

"Are you not going to welcome our tourists to the town Paul? God love them sitting down over there behind you, they're probably waiting for table service. Be a long fucking wait for them God bless them. But don't worry Paulo you'll always come first in my eyes so here you are, one nice pint of milk!"

Paul went into his pocket for his wallet and flicked past the receipts and his photo of James until he found the single crisp €50 he was searching for.

"Give me a pint of lager, a bottle of lager and a glass of red as well there Charlie" Paul asked "for the family."

"Jesus Paul is that Maura and the kids? I wouldn't have picked them out of a line-up!" Charlie was asking Paul as she poured the pint and opened the bottle with her free hand, proving that she could actually multi-task and work fast now and again.

"Louise had her graduation there today so we went out for a bite and then decided to stop in for a quick pint on the way home."

Charlene got Paul's change from the till and leaned in close as she handed it over, "are you planning on having a chat with them while you're here?"

"That's the plan anyway but I'm terrified of it, I need this Dutch courage to get me started I think. Thanks love" he said moving towards the table with the two pints.

Charlene watched him move, looking for all the world like a condemned man. Just as his arse was about to touch the uncomfortably low seat Maura leant in to him with the ¼ bottle of red. Charlie stayed where she was. "Sorry Charlie can I swap this for a white instead?" was all he said but Charlie could read from his hunched shoulders and frowned face so much more about how he was feeling about the task ahead. She didn't know what she could possibly say so simply went with silence and made the exchange.

Paul caught her hand as she picked up the red wine. "Ironic isn't it? She hasn't drunk red wine in about 20 years. Just shows you where my mind is tonight." Paul managed a grin of sorts as he turned and sloped back to his family.

Charlie stood watching him walk the ten feet but then felt she might be prying so she wandered down to the bottom of the pub and the 3 degenerates inhabiting that area of the world. She sat back against the back counter so while she couldn't hear the conversation she could still see the Forsyth's at their table when she glanced their way.

She thought back on the tragic story Paul had unloaded on her last Sunday. She couldn't help but feel sorry for Paul but she felt more pity for Maura and the kids. Paul had dealt with his grief in his own way. It was the wrong way but he'd done something. 'How has Maura coped with such loss and secrecy over the years? And what about the two kids? Jesus they'd no inkling of the bombshell about to be dropped on them. And the poor girl, she'll never forget her graduation day anyway. But probably not for the reasons she thought.'

"Oi! Soppy head! Give us a pint will you I'm gasping!" Charlie was brought back to earth with the clever wit of a regular customer. She composed herself and began to pour his pint without saying a word.

Meanwhile just 30 feet away, Paul was squirming in his seat. It wasn't HIS stool at the counter and it was a low seat but the squirming was all about figuring out how to begin what he wanted to say. He'd tried to practice some sort of speech all day but each and every time he started at a different point in the story. He was fidgety and anxious and he was patting his pockets and rubbing his nose, simply to be doing something with his hands, then he hit it in his last pocket.

As he tapped the disposable camera he knew where to begin. He wasn't about to take a drink from his pint before he'd completed his 'prayers' over the stout. So the condensation stayed untouched on the side of the glass and Paul just began. As he took the camera out of his pocket he said, "I know you were really embarrassed by me taking out this camera earlier but it's going to help me say what I've got to say........."

34.

Paul placed the camera in the middle of the small pub table. It sat there alone and silent; a relic of times past. Jack and Louise were alternating between staring at it, at each other and at their father. Minds racing with the endless thoughts of what their father might be about to tell them. None came close to the truth at all. Even Maura sat staring at the camera. Slowly the realisation dawned on her what exactly Paul was about to do.

"Paul?" she whispered, "is this really the time and the place to do this?"

"I think it's just got to be done. I spend so much time here that I feel comfortable to talk. I wonder is it the low, cramped ceiling, the dim lights or the alcohol that provides refuge from the cruel world outside." Paul tried to force a chuckle but it was beyond him.

Louise and Jack's eyes now began to dart from their father to their mother to the table to the exit. The safe and easy escape route.

"What the fuck is going on?" Jack asked, assuming the responsibility as big brother. "There's something big going on and you're going to have to tell us now you've started. Maura's eyes began to fill with tears and seeing this Jack turned towards his father for answers.

"I'm going to drink this pint for you James. I'm going to enjoy it and I'm going to think of you as I do." Slowly, deliberately Paul began to wipe the condensation from his glass. "I will never, ever forget you and please give me the strength to tell the kids what I'm about to." Raising the glass towards his lip he added, "God rest you

James and keep you safe now and forever." With that blessing, Paul downed half his pint, paying tribute to his son the only way he knew how.

Maura had begun to sob and her shoulders rocked with each passing wave of emotion. Louise reached out and took her hand; sitting beside her mother she was closest to hand.

"Whatever this is Mam; we can get over it or through it, won't we?" Louise asked.

Jack was sitting beside his father but could barely look at him never mind offer comfort to a man he didn't know. Instead he pointed out, "James is the name Mam called me the other day. So what the fuck is going on here? Tell us exactly what ye are talking about."

"You're right son the time has come to tell you both the truth. Your mother and I have lived with a terrible secret for 24 years and now we need to tell you so that we can begin to heal properly. Patricia O'Neill died 3 weeks ago in a tragic accident..."

"What in the name of fuck has that got to do with anything Dad? What's that got to do with you and Mam?"

"I'll tell you Jack, I'll tell you now but it's going to be hard and I don't know how to say it so please, please let me speak. When Patricia died it was a terrible tragedy that affected the whole community. A little white coffin has got to be one of the saddest sights to witness in this world. When I went to the funeral, a lot of memories were evoked and that's why I've been so short and moody these last few weeks."

Louise was by now snuggled in to her mother's side and tried desperately to keep the tone light. "That explains the last few weeks Da but what about before then?!" Paul forced a grimace at his daughters' dig but carried on. He knew she was right. "When Patricia died I was reminded of what happened in June 1990. AND that is where the disposable camera comes in too. In those days rolls of film and disposable cameras were the only options for taking pictures. No digital cameras then and it was on a disposable camera I took this photo." Paul fished in his wallet for the photo of James that had been seen and handled by more people this week than in the previous 24 years. "This is a picture of James Forsyth. He would've been your older brother had......had he not died on the 11th June 1990."

****

To say Jack and Louise were stunned was the understatement of the year, decade probably. They both looked wide eyed at the photo, each other and then their parents. Their mouths wide open, their minds racing with a million and one questions. What had happened? How come they'd never heard about this boy? Why were they being told now?
Maura squeezed Louise even closer; grateful to have someone to hold and comfort, grateful for the opportunity to be there for her daughter when Louise needed her most. She looked across the table at Jack and wondered what to do. She could see he was shocked, she could see he was hurt at being lied to; she could see his heart was breaking and she could see that, despite his

best efforts, tears poured forth from his eyes as he tried to fight the news alone. Maura recognised all this because this is exactly what she and Paul had taught him to do subconsciously all his life.

"Are you alright son?" she asked gingerly. "Yeah Mam, I'm grand, I'm fine, I'm just a bit……" he took a huge breath in and tried to bite off the grief, " I'm grand, just a bit shocked ya know?". He was lying and used the back of his hand to wipe away his tears to prove that. These were tears he couldn't control. Tears for someone he'd never met but missed desperately at the same time.

"Jack love will you get me some tissues from the bathroom please?" Maura asked her son, knowing that although he was ostensibly going for tissues that weren't needed, he would take the opportunity to compose himself and dry his eyes a little. As he returned to the table, Maura was happy to see he had done just that. Paul meanwhile, sipped away at his pint. Because he was in control, and knew this topic of conversation would be brought up by him, he was prepared. He didn't notice the depth of emotion the revelation had elicited.

Jack sat back down on the inside of the table. He sat on the long bench under the window on the other side of his mother to Louise. He sat there and allowed her put her arm around him and pull him close. He felt so much more comfortable there, in the protective surrounds of his mother's embrace. Easier to sit like that than to try and get comfort from his Dad. 'How would that go?' he thought, 'a handshake? A pat on the back? Just a glance?'

"I'm glad you've sat in there son." Paul continued "we're all going to need to support and comfort each other over the next while and you kids know I'm not very good at doing this."

Paul picked up the camera, once again, and read the instructions and other gibberish written on its' sides. "As I said this photo was taken on a disposable camera on the 11th June 1990. James is 3 and ½ years old and I've carried it around in my wallet ever since to remember him. We had James when we were quite young. We were living further north at the time. I was absolutely terrified of doing the wrong thing with him. I was afraid I'd hurt him or drop him or something. I couldn't find a way to bond with him. Your mother, as she has been for you two, was amazing though, a more natural mother you couldn't find.

So anyway, this one night in June I decided I'd take James to the park............"

Paul continued speaking for a solid ten minutes. He recounted the argument, the man who took the photo, the accident and the aftermath. Maura had re-run those events time and time again and managed to maintain her composure as Paul spoke. She had grieved many times over for James and cried her eyes out far too often. On this occasion, she knew she had to keep it together for her children's sake. She held them close, one under each arm, a mother protecting her vulnerable young.

Jack and Louise, meanwhile, maintained a shocked silence. Neither of them had had even the merest inkling of anything like this in their family history. 'What's the appropriate response to hearing that someone you've never heard of died 24 years ago? Is there an appropriate response?' Jack's mind was doing somersaults, 'how cool would it have been to have an older brother though?'

"……… so naturally enough I've been thinking about James a lot recently, thinking about James but also about Mr. O'Neill. I know exactly what he is going through and it must be so rough on him.

So last night as I passed the chemists James told me to go in and pick up a camera. The time was right to create new memories with you pair. You know full well I'm not religious but he spoke to me last night. He reminded me how much I love this photo and how it's high time you know the truth."

Louise was, surprisingly, first to speak. Even though it took some time, Paul was instantly proud of her strength and her character. He had hit his two children with a torrent of emotion and an avalanche of information. He noticed her words were very matter of fact, but maybe that was shock. "That's some secret for you both to hold between you for so long. I've no idea how you've done it and stayed together all this time but I hope you feel better for acknowledging the truth."

"It's been tough Louise, very tough in fact" Maura responded picking her words very carefully. "I wish you had warned me you were planning this Paul. But definitely it feels better that you both now know the truth."

"Jesus Dad, you never checked with Mam before telling us?" Jack was incredulous. "You really live in your own little world don't you?"

Maura interrupted to defend her husband, something she had years of practice doing. "Listen it was always going to be hard to talk about this and I think if your father had told me about his plans I might have tried to dissuade him."

"But still Mam?"

"But still nothing Jack." Maura was firm but compassionate in her tone. "That's what happened and unfortunately we can't change any of it. It's what we say when I go up to the bereavement counselling meetings on a Monday; 'death is always a shock, no matter how expected or unexpected it is. The important thing is to try and move on through the difficult emotions.'"

"You mean you're not just the counsellor Mam?" Louise spat out.

"No love I'm not, I'm one of the participants as well."

"And all this time I thought you had set up the group as a way to help other people."

"No I go along to tell my story, talk to other parents who've lost children and spend some time with people who understand what we're going through. There are parents there who lost young children or when they were adult children. Some of them have had late miscarriages. It doesn't matter what the actual background is, the emotions and feelings are pretty much all the same; loss, grief, guilt, sadness at missing out on the future. It really is an awful tragedy to befall anyone."

"Have you ever gone to these sessions Dad?" Jack presumed he wasn't but he wanted to see if his Dad was open to that sort of thing.

"Ah jaysus I did at the beginning son but it wasn't for me. I felt the people there were wallowing and grieving continuously. They never seemed to move on to the getting better phase so I stopped going. I decided I'd have to process James' death myself, my own way and somehow carry on."

"And how has that worked out for you?"

"Not very well to tell the truth son. I am an angry, guilt-ridden man and I cannot have you thinking that is me anymore."

35.

Stunned. Shocked. Dumbstruck. Amazed. Louise, just
two weeks shy of her Leaving Certificate English paper,
had synonyms racing through her mind. She heard Jack
ask a couple of questions but didn't hear the answers.
She herself was unable to speak at all. Her first thought
of many was of herself and then almost immediately she
felt guilty for thinking that way. 'How can Dad think this
is the time to reveal something as monumental as this?
My exams are so soon and he'll expect me to concentrate
on them with this on my mind?'
Not unlike her parents, Louise has a very quick guilt
trigger. A single half-thought, honest reaction was
enough to start her off. She wouldn't ever consider
saying anything about her exams. But this shared trait of
guilt finally allowed her to summon up the courage to
speak. If she felt like that about a selfish thought, how
the hell must her parents have felt then? Or now even?
"Dad, how in the hell did that happen? More
importantly, how did you cope? And you Mam? How
did you both cope with such a tragedy? And then how
did you cope with keeping it a secret? It's just
unbelievable, isn't it Jack?" A single nod from an open-
mouthed Jack confirmed he was thinking the same thing.
"That's the thing kids, there are going to be lots of
answers that you need answers to and we'll try and do
that for you. The 'How did it happen?' question still
slays me to this day. That's the biggest cause of guilt for
me." Paul turned away before continuing, "he was in my

care and he died because I didn't watch him carefully enough."

Maura pulled her children still closer and with tears streaming down her face, she squeezed them tight and repeated the mantra she's said to Paul so often, "accidents can happen and unfortunately they do happen. It could've happened at any time to anybody."

"But it was on my watch and to alleviate some of my own guilt I did the worst thing I've ever done in my entire life."

"You don't need to Paul"

"Yes I do. I blamed your mother kids and I didn't just think it, I lashed out at your mam and told her she had to take some of the blame."

Jack and Louise turned away from their mothers' side in unison so that Paul could feel their eyes burning into him. He had his eyes lowered to his pint but he could feel their gaze, afraid to catch their eyes.

"For fucks sake Dad! How the fuck could you do that? You were both grieving and you tried to lay blame at Mam's door? How could you do that?" Jack was furious but managed to control himself so that this rebuke came out in an aggressive whisper, so much so that the other 5 customers were still oblivious to the crisis meeting taking place in their midst. Jack wanted answers but he didn't expect the next voice he heard to be his mothers.

"Grief makes you do some things that in the cold light of day seem inexplicable. Your Dad only ever said that once, twice at most, in the first few days after James died. It was shock, pure and simple. We just needed to be there for each other more than ever. We'd no family

to fall back on for support so we had to rely on each other. We made mistakes but we were all we had."
"Your mother is an exceptional woman kids, but you already know that. You told me you forgave me almost immediately but I've never forgiven myself. It's something I continue to beat myself up over."
"How could you do that Mam? You're so sensitive and yet you forgave him for the absolute worst thing he could ever say?" Louise couldn't bring herself to look at Paul as she spoke.
"We were both in such deep shock and on complete auto-pilot that we just got on with things without thinking too much about anything we said or did."
"But did no one step up to help you out or guide you in anyway?"
The local priest was about all we had. Both sets of our parents were already dead and as you know we're single children so there were no siblings to pitch in. So we left a lot of the arrangements to the Priest and he just guided us from ceremony to ceremony really for the first few weeks."
"But why didn't you tell anyone? Why have you kept it from us and everyone else?" Louise was really struggling to get her head around their mind-set.
"Well, with no family to talk to that was pretty straight forward and we sleep-walked through our lives for ages." Maura began.
"Yeah, like we never had a conversation about not telling anyone," Paul took over. "We just found ourselves at Christmas in 1990 with no one calling on us or checking how we were. That Christmas was awful, absolutely soul destroying. It was just so quiet. I'd kind

of hoped that by then we'd have begun to feel somewhat normal but things were just as raw. Everyone in Ardee knew us so they'd be pointing and whispering and then offering the dopey 'I'm sorry' face when you passed them. It was just constant reminders."

"But were there no professionals to help? No doctor's to tell you to talk about what you'd been through?" Jack asked.

"No not in those days son. It's not the dark ages but 1990 was a different world. Nobody talked about their feelings or the like. Nobody spoke to counsellors or anything. If you had an issue or a fight in your marriage, you just knuckled down and toughed it out. If it happened today, every, and all, –ologists in the world would want to get inside your head but back then we just carried on."

"But the priest or the church must have been a good support. They must've been Mam, if you're still going to the groups?" Jack asked.

"It was for your mother for a time but I couldn't cope with it. My thoughts were always that 'how could a God let something like that happen to good people like us?'" The importance of Paul's question hung in the air for several moments before Maura spoke.

"It's amazing how strong the mind can be and how important it is when you're in shock. I've considered the same question your Dad just asked many, many times myself. I cried and I cried and I screamed at an unanswering God on many long nights when I couldn't sleep. But the one constant through all the years of my grief has been the Church. They are always there for me, I've never been judged and I know there is a reason for everything that has happened.

Over time I've come to believe that God doesn't give us anything to deal with that we can't manage. We had done nothing wrong, it's not like we deserved for this to happen. God knew we were strong enough to cope with the death of a child and for what it's worth I think we've done alright."

"What a load of complete and utter rubbish!" Paul exclaimed before putting another big hole in his pint. Maura felt the strength of her children empowering her and she steeled herself for the coming 'discussion', the same one they'd been having on and off for 24 years. "Just because you don't believe something doesn't make it wrong Paul. I choose to believe that God has a plan greater than our comprehension. We're still together after all this time so yes, I do believe we are strong as a unit and we've been strong enough to cope with a lot."

"Well I suppose there's no denying that Maura" Paul said as he reached across the table to take her hand before she picked up her glass. Jack and Louise looked at each other behind their mother's back, amazed at the physical contact between their parents. For the first time realising, that they weren't immaculate conceptions and there was a time when their parents enjoyed a little intimacy.

"You don't believe Paul but I do and all those who turn up in the church on a Monday evening believe too. I would've loved more support from you over the years but I had to get it somewhere. Better to do that than for us to have gone our separate ways." Paul kept his hand on Maura's and gave a gentle squeeze. A flood of emotions and reminders of the love and affection they had for each other washed over them. Even though they didn't show it very often, it was there.

Paul raised his glass before him, "correct me if I go wrong Maura; Take this pint all of you and drink it. This is the pint glass of our salvation and everyone who drinks from it will feel like they can live forever (but may not remember it) Amen!" Paul drained his glass and hoped that his family could laugh, even a little, through the tears in their eyes; anything to release the tension and emotions. "You have your God and I have mine. You have your church and I have mine, except my church allows women priests! Charlene?" Paul rose to get another round in.

"Looks like your 'priest' knows you too well Paul!" Maura said as she pointed in Charlie's direction as she brought over another round. Although Maura noted this was probably not a regular occurrence judging by how uncomfortable she was carrying the tray.

Charlie felt even more uncomfortable holding the tray than she looked to Maura. Yes she'd been a barmaid for years but The Local never went all in for Bar of the Year. As a result Charlene NEVER dropped drinks over to customers but knowing what the Forsyth's were going through, she was willing to make an exception.

"Here you go" Charlie said gruffly as she slammed the shaking tray on to the table spilling some of the pints. As she exchanged the new glasses for the old she said, "I thought yis looked like yis needed another round. So there you go, and don't get any ideas Paul, they're not on the house so you can square up with me later, right?"

"Yeah absolutely Charlie thanks for doing that for us." He considered touching her hand as she picked up the last empty glass but changed his mind and picked up his pint instead.

Jack watched his father caress his pint with the outside of his little finger. He was removing the condensation as he always did but though Jack had seen him do it many times; he'd never actually asked his father about it.

"Why do you do that Dad? Is it to make the pint look better or what?"

"It's partly that alright son but there's more to it than just that. It's my little ritual, my blessing for want of a better description. I just take a second to bow my head a little, say a little message to James and ask him to look out for us. It also passes the time between getting the pint and it settling fully so you can drink it so I'll leave you to decide which is the real reason!"

****

It was a huge shock for Jack and Louise to hear about someone they'd never even known of, who would've been there big brother, to hear about the accident and then figure out how they should respond or grieve for someone in those circumstances. Jack shifted away from his mother just a little bit as he considered his next move. He looked at his sister still tucked under their mother's protective wing and decided he needed to show he could get over his own shock and look after his little sister.

"I'm not sure what you expect from us or expect us to do after telling us this news. Were you expecting us to bawl crying? Did you expect us to storm out of here? Did you expect us to feel guilty if we can't grieve properly for someone we've never known? 'Cos I can't do that. I'm mostly upset for you two. My emotion and tears are for what you two have gone through rather than grief for a lost brother. What you two have been through is heart-breaking. I really don't know how you kept it to yourselves all these years. I feel bad that you didn't feel you could tell us sooner. I think I'm speaking for both of us, right Lou?, when I say we'll try to be more understanding and now that we know, maybe you can talk to us a little more too?"

Jack and Louise had their moments as siblings but underneath it all they were incredibly protective and supportive of each other. As Jack finished his little speech, Louise looked up and nodded gently at Jack, grateful that he had expressed what she was thinking too. Paul put down his pint and looked at Maura. "What did I tell you earlier love? Didn't I tell you you'd done a great job raising these kids? I'm so proud of both of you tonight and the young adults you've become thanks to your mother's efforts. I'd love to say we were both equally responsible for raising you but your mother did all the heavy lifting. I threw myself into work and drinking when you both were born and I'll be eternally guilty of that. It's eaten away at me but I've known, even though I'd never see you short of anything, I've never been completely available to you. I was always terrified that I'd let something similar happen to you if I had the same responsibility so I passed the buck and backed away from it all."

"Bloody hell Dad, this has obviously taken so much from you over the years, have you ever even grieved properly for your son's loss?" Louise felt so sorry for her father as he broke down before their eyes. "You've struggled on for so long but why tell us now, why all the rush to tell us the truth about what happened?"

"I've wanted to tell you both for a long time but there just never seemed to be a good time you know?"

"So you picked Louise's graduation night? Is that good timing Dad?"

"No Jack it's definitely not but it had to be done. Patricia O'Neill's death dragged up a lot of stuff for us both and then your graduation and the possibility of you moving to Cork for college became real Louise. And you won't be living with us forever either Jack, despite what you might want to think! So I suppose I was afraid. I.... was...... afraid......afraid that...."

"Go ahead Paul, you can do this. Tell them what you said to me the other night. You can do this and you'll feel better for it."

"I was afraid kids, terrified in fact. I didn't want you both moving out thinking I was an uncaring, emotionless and selfish man. I love you both very, very much but I'm afraid to go all in, just in case I lose you too. If I let myself become closer with you two than I was with James and anything had happened, it would have hurt even more and it would've been the end of me I think." That's why I've seemed so distant and harsh and uncaring all these years. I feel so guilty admitting this to you both but I was so afraid of losing you I didn't get to know and spend time with you growing up."

"Jesus Christ Dad! We were just getting up off the canvas after hearing about our brother and you slap us back down with another massive body-blow?" Jack reached for his pint and drank down about a third of the way, exactly the way Paul did when he was angry.

Charlie watched this scene play out; she was beyond earshot but wondered how they were doing. 'It's hard to put yourself out there, even to those you love, about your past mistakes isn't it Charlene? Will you ever have the strength to do the same yourself?'

36.

'What are you so fuckin' worried about? It's as simple as fuck. Look at Paul down there, if he can do it then why the fuck can't you?' Charlie stood against the fridges watching Paul and Maura talk to their children but she mostly watched Paul.

He'd drunk in here as long as she had worked in The Local. He wasn't one of her friends who drank there but he wasn't one of the dickheads either. He had 30 years on her, all of her life pretty much, so they struggled to find common ground. But he'd always been relatively polite to Charlie. As polite as any man in his 50's could be to a younger girl working in a pub. She presumed he viewed her as beneath him and subservient, not through anything intentional, merely a result of the generation he belonged to.

Another trait common in men of that age that Charlie served in the pub was stoicism. Everything and anything even resembling an emotion was either dismissed or pushed down deep inside and buried under a sea of stout. That was the way the world worked. Or at least that was how Charlie had thought it worked.

She had been watching in awe for nearly half an hour as Paul laid himself bare in front of her. He was sacrificing everything he'd done to build a protective space for himself in The Local. He was prostrating himself in front of his family and begging their forgiveness and understanding. He had brought them inside his sanctuary and broken down the walls. Hopeful that somehow they could be rebuilt as something stronger.

Charlie could merely watch no longer. She spotted their drinks were all well past half finished, and so set about preparing the same round of drinks for the Forsyths. Charlie felt partly compelled to do so out of respect but also out of a desire not to force a break in their moment. She was also driven by something else too. She couldn't completely believe her eyes and wanted to interact with the Forsyths and make sure what was happening wasn't a wild fantasy concocted in her head.

"Don't be expecting this all the time and you can square up with me later, before you leave Paul." She had said while transferring the glasses but what she heard was astounding. Paul really was laying out the chain of events that had brought his family to this point. 'The kids, she thought, are taking it well too. Either they are purely in shock or Maura has done a great job bringing them up. For all the time he spends in here and the stories he tells, I doubt Paul has ever been a fully hands-on father.'

Charlie floated to the bottom of the counter and served the few customers gathered in the rejects corner on autopilot. Pouring cheap lagers and even cheaper 'vodka' that was the staple diet of the clientele down there didn't take much concentration.

This was very lucky for Charlie as her brain was rushing all over the place. She could feel the muscles on top of her shoulders and in her neck pulsing and tightening up. The adrenaline was certainly flowing and as Mrs. Raftery used to say. 'The blood was up.' It had been a long time since she had thought of Mrs. Raftery and yet here she was just as Charlie was caught in a fight or flight moment. Seeing Paul face up to his demons, put her in mind of her own struggles and issues of 15 years before. She could feel Derek's oppressive presence on her once again.

She ran over everything she had said that day, just like she had done thousands of times, wondering if she really HAD said something or done something, anything, to lead Derek on or make him feel that he had to take her virginity that awful day. She also saw in her mind's eye, her sweet, delicate mother and felt ashamed of all the lies she had told her right up until the moment of her death.

"Is there something you would like to tell me Charlene? I don't have long left so if you want to tell me anything now is the time."

"There's nothing at all that you don't know already Mam, just remember that I love you with all my heart and I'm going to miss you terribly. I don't know how to go on without you Mam."

Charlie also thought back on the trips to Dublin and beyond, the lies she had had to tell so many people. Those lies which she now believed to be true as she'd told so often to teachers and friends who had guessed that something was up. These were teachers and friends she had cruelly pushed away in case she told any of them the truth.

The truth she had buried deep within her for years. The truth she had kept from her mother. The truth that had shattered her confidence. The truth that left her happy to settle for life in a rural town. The truth she feared thinking about. The truth that had led her to be bitter and tough when, deep down, she was a sensitive and delicate young girl. The truth that meant she too had built walls to protect herself. The truth that turned her into a cold, seemingly heartless barmaid who was strong and stern when working. The truth that had destroyed any chance of letting friends get close to her. The truth that made her fearful of all men who showed any interest. Fearful of her safety, fearful for her future and fearful of her reputation being ruined by the release of a long-held secret.

'Are you going to run away from the truth once more? Push it down to the pit of your stomach once more? Let it feed your anger, bitterness and isolation? Or are you going to follow Paul's example? Can you choose to unburden yourself? Can you choose how and when people found out what had happened? Can you choose to face down Derek and his evil threats? Can you, in telling the truth, turn the judgement onto Derek and off yourself?'

"You're damn fucking right I do!" Charlie blurted out as she served a pint of Fosters. A more evolved human might have wondered why Charlie was talking to herself but that evolution hadn't happened for Whacker so he wondered if he had asked Charlie a question without noticing.

Charlie could feel the adrenaline coursing through her veins and all doubt had been erased from her mind about what was going to happen. Impressed by Paul and how a man of his generation could acknowledge his emotions, Charlie had reached a decision about her own life and situation. She was filled with a desire to fight, to fight for herself which was something she hadn't done enough of over the years.

'I'm gonna have to tell everyone about the abortion I had when I was 17. I'm gonna have to tell them all that it was a horrible, yet vital, decision to make because of what that bastard rapist did to me. Do you know in fifteen years that is the first time you've referred to Derek as that Charlie? But that is exactly what he did and he is. It wasn't your fault, you are the innocent one and it's time for the truth to be told. It's time to free yourself of the guilt of being another young country Irish girl willing to travel to England for an abortion.

37.

"I'll tell you another one for the price of a pint! I've got fucking loads of those stories and old tales. Spending years working alongside all them labourers and builders, you pick up things. I mean I've lived my life but those lads? Jesus Christ they'll skid backwards into their graves at a 100mph!"

Revolving on his high bar stool, Derek took in his surroundings and his audience. Here he was in all his pomp and glory. Thursday afternoon was Pensioners Pint day in The Local, but for the chance to spend his hard-earned benefits on a cheaper than normal pint, Derek could make an exception.

All the older heads from Kilcastle drank in The Local throughout the week and they didn't need to give out any extra incentives to get punters in the door. But the fact that they went ahead and did it anyway was very much appreciated by the regulars. They turned up in great numbers to enjoy the cheaper pints, cheaper but just as good they always said. They also got to enjoy the craic and company of their peers without the youngsters interrupting them. Within a short period of time, Thursday afternoons in The Local became not to be missed events. A chance to gossip, laugh, judge and slander the residents of the town.

'They wouldn't have done that in our day', closely followed by 'another pint there Charlene' were the most common utterances on a Thursday. It was a relaxed, laid back atmosphere in the pub and whoever pulled the afternoon shift didn't really mind as it was 99% stout there was never the chance of a cross word being spoken, never any sort of difficulty. Everybody in the town respected the OAP's day to themselves. Well they used to anyway.

Unfortunately the atmosphere had begun to change and not for the better. Derek Flynn was back in the town and the new element added to the pub's Thursday afternoon chemistry. And as Charlie knew all too well, he could be a human wrecking ball with his carry on.

He had barged back into her life three months earlier. He strolled into the pub one random Thursday afternoon, nice as pie and acting like he'd left the town on a week's holiday not for good 12/13 years before. Charlie had instantly been frozen to the spot and felt numb with shock at the physical reminder and link to her past life.

All the younger folk in the town knew that Thursday afternoon in The Local wasn't a welcoming place for anyone not an OAP. Most wouldn't dream of setting foot inside the door and those that did picked up very quickly that while they'd never be told to leave they weren't very welcome gate-crashing this particular party.

In all his life Derek had never cared or worried about what other people thought of him. He did things that made him happy and had the thickest skin for smart comments. That was why he was still there on a Thursday afternoon 3 months later. Still telling them stories they didn't want to hear. Still getting under everyone's skin and enjoying every minute of it.

As Derek turned back to face the bar counter, he asked Charlie for another pint. She gave him her best look of cold, detachment. She didn't really know how she was going to show Derek her new found strength but she wanted to give him the hint that he no longer made her nervous and held control over here. Derek Flynn was nothing and meant nothing at all to her and soon everybody would know that. She only wished she'd had the strength to do so 3 months ago but better late than never she thought.

Shocked and afraid of what Derek knew and could reveal about to the moral conscience of the town, Charlie had served him just like anybody else when he strolled into the pub and she answered all his questions about different people and what had happened in the town over the past 12 years.

Most of the lads sitting in The Local that day had recognised Derek when he walked back into their lives. Those that didn't recognise him were soon put straight by those sitting around them. They reminded each other of the local toe-rag who had terrorised the residents of the town with his carrying on as a teenager.

Somebody with a rap sheet like his would normally be giving the cold shoulder treatment from the lads and run out of the pub. They were a self-policing group but when they saw Charlie give him the time of day and then pour him a pint they trusted her that she was ok with his presence. So instead of giving him the evil eye until he left, they let him stay and enjoy his few pints. But by now they too had had enough of the one-man shows. Charlie placed Derek's pint in front of him without a word. She made sure to catch his eye though. She wanted to stare at him and if possible through him. "What's with the frosty the snowman act today Charlie?" He leaned in closer to whisper his next question, "time of the month or something?" He then winked at her in that sleazy way he'd done for years. But Charlie wasn't going to rise to the bait today. She slapped his coins back on to the counter without answering either question. Swivelling round again, bored at not getting a reaction from Charlie, Derek faced the customers who were happily swapping stories of the latest old codger to kick the metaphorical bucket or lose their marbles. They were all happy for the chance to share a little gossip, while being grateful that neither fate had befallen them.

"For fuck's sake lads, yis better take it easy with our Charlene today. She's a little highly strung and liable to lash out over the slightest little bit of banter." Derek spread his arms as he spoke, trying to draw as many people as possible into his show but they weren't giving him a big enough response so he decided to try again, a little louder this time. "I know your hearing aids mightn't be turned up to full but I said, tread carefully with Charlie today, she's a little what will we call it 'hormonal' this afternoon s try not to wind her up."

"For fuck's sake Derek, give it a rest will you. We heard you the first time but you're not quite the comedian you think you are. No one ever invited you in here on a Thursday afternoon, did they?"

"Good man George thanks for standing up for me, as always, but I've got this one covered."

"If you're sure darling?" George was the only man who called her by any form of nickname and could get away with calling her darling but even he was already sitting down and knew full well Charlie could fight her own battles if needs be.

"I'm sure George." And she was. She felt more certain of that than many things in her life before. Paul had inspired her and Derek had pushed her once too often. The time had come to remove any guilt she felt from her story. Derek was going to get the comeuppance he deserved.

38.

The noise of the bell ringing echoed around the low ceilings of the pub. The loudest noise ever heard in The Local, was quickly followed by the longest silence. Everyone knew that the bell existed but they also presumed that it was never rung. It was a relic of times past, a 'last-call' bell that time had forgotten. Suddenly and violently everybody knew it was fully functional. Nobody whispered about what was going on. The local OAP's were stunned into silence and even those who did indeed have their hearing aids switched off had no problem hearing the bell ringing.

Charlie stood completely stock-still. Her right hand held fast to the bell rope as the reverberations continued around her, her left hand was planted on her hip, partly to show she meant business but more importantly to avoid her shaking hand to be seen. Every sense was heightened, she had tried to block all feelings of touch and excitement for many years but now she stood in her safest place feeling every tingle in her body, feeling the strength flow to her extremities until her toes and fingers pulsed.

Derek was the first to break the silence.

"Fucking hell Charlie, you could have given the old lads a bit of warning before giving them a heart attack. I mean they'd have got a smaller heart attack if you were working topless for the afternoon, I mean...."

"Shut the fuck up Derek and while I'm at it sit the fuck down. George and his mates don't like me using bad language but they'll forgive me this time." Charlie

pointed an accusatory finger at Derek before continuing,
"sit the fuck down and listen for once in your miserable,
petty life." Charlie wasn't as loud as she had begun but
her steely resolve shone through every word.
"Gents it's past time we, sorry I, enforced the rules of the
Thursday club. We only have the two rules so it
shouldn't be hard but I've been too relaxed about them.
You're either old enough to qualify or you took early
retirement and so are on a pension too. Over the last
while someone who doesn't satisfy either of these
conditions has been allowed sit amongst you. This of
course is that fucking waste of space Derek Flynn and
I'd be surprised if anyone volunteers to speak up on his
behalf."
"You have to work to get a pension don't you George?"
Charlie asked but George knew well enough to stay quiet
and not interrupt Charlie's flow. "But what have you
ever done to justify that perk? Sweet fuck all is what!
You don't belong here Derek, nobody wants you to be
here and while these lads will never say it directly to
you, I'm going to do it for them; Pick up your coat, your
shitty stack of coins and get out! And what's more don't
even think about coming back in here again."
Charlie had moved down the counter as she spoke and
now found herself up close and personal with Derek with
just the width of the bar counter between them. She had
her hands splayed on the counter praying they wouldn't
betray her real fears. Derek leaned in close and
whispering, he raked over the old coals of his threats and
bullying tactics.
"You forget Charlene, that I can ruin your reputation in
this town in an instant. You don't get to tell me what to

do because I hold all the aces and it'll take nothing for me to show everyone my winning hand."

"If you're going to threaten me Derek, at least keep your voice up so everyone can hear what you've got to say for yourself. Sorry folks, sorry to disturb you again but Derek here has something he'd like to share with the whole class. Go ahead Derek; you've everyone's attention now so tell them what you just said to me."

Derek eyed her up and down but Charlie's resolve was well formed and he couldn't see the chink in her armour. She didn't look she was going to fold this time and he began to consider the fact that his race might be run. He didn't surrender though, like wave after wave of soldiers going over the top, he knew he had to go out swinging.

"You wouldn't dare let me speak out like that Charlie, would you? Let me tell these lovely people how you're nothing more than a tramp, a slut who got herself into trouble when she didn't know what was good for her."

Her eyes and stance told Derek to try her. "I'm laughing at the idea of Charlie trying to bar me. I know her better than anyone and we go back a very long way. She's never been able to fight her way out of a wet paper bag so she's not going to start now. I'm not going anywhere, in fact Charlie's about to put me on another pint."

"I'm not you know. The days of you threatening me are over. When we were kids, just 17 in fact, we went out for a very short time. We all make mistakes in life and that was one of mine, the second was regressing to the timid schoolgirl I was when you walked back in here 3 months ago.

I spent days, weeks, months after you left, crying my eyes out about what you did to me and what you forced me to do. I cried myself to sleep at night, wishing I'd never have to see you again. I told no one, I confided in no one. I spent my days caring for my mam until the day she was put out of her misery. Bit by tiny bit, as the months became years I felt like I was just beginning to move on. I'll never be able to forget what you did but as time passed, my dreams were haunted less and less by your face. And then bang!" Charlie's hand slammed on to the counter for effect. Still no one else spoke and the echo continued.

"Then three months ago you strolled back in here with not a care in the world. We were 17, we were carefree and we were unaware of the real difficulties life can throw at us. Well I was young and naïve; you were a cold-hearted, calculating prick. You may have thought you were more worldly wise but underneath you were, and you still are, a frightened little boy trying to assert your dominance over those you think are weaker. I was weaker but not anymore.

Derek and I went out for about a month when we were 17. I wanted my first time to be special and Derek had been with other girls so I hoped he'd be able to guide me. One day he arrived into my house thinking we were going to sleep together that day. I wasn't ready and I told him that, again and again, but Derek wasn't going to be put off." Gentle tears rolled down Charlie's cheeks as she told the assembled congregation her story, as she showed them vulnerability they didn't know she had. "That day changed my life for ever. Derek bullied and coerced me into getting what he wanted, despite my protestations, and then he left me there.

He left me there to suffer, to feel humiliated and ashamed. I had to get to Dublin myself to make sure I couldn't be pregnant. Then I had to go to England when I was actually pregnant. I had to stay at home with Mam instead of going to college, I took a job in this pub so I could have some control, and I was never able to move out of my family home or spread my wings outside this town. You forced me to distrust any man that dared to show me any kindness. You forced me to fear living in the place I grew up in. It happened in my own home and if it could happen there, where I felt safest, then it could happen again anywhere.

You ruined my life you selfish bastard. You ruined my life and then left without a thought. And just when I might be getting to a point where I could live with myself, you return to try and destroy me all over again. I'm not going to let that happen, I can't afford to let that happen. So fuck you and what you did to my life!

But it stops now. No more threatening, no more blackmail, no more intimidating me. Just get the fuck out of this pub and keep going until you're out of my life for good!"

Charlie had summoned the last of her strength to deliver these last lines with as much force as she could muster. But once the words had left her mouth, the adrenaline began to leave her body too. She sank back against the fridges behind her, her silent tears kept falling and her hands shook and shook. Very soon the enormity of what she had done would envelope her but not just yet. She needed to see things through first.

Derek, meanwhile, sat stunned and silent on his stool. He found himself staring at his shoes, praying for a way to respond. All the power and control he had ever held over Charlie was gone. No longer could he manipulate and bully her.

After what seemed like an age to all the customers in The Local, Derek raised his eyes from the floor and opened his mouth to say something, anything. But he had nothing left to offer, no quick comment, no joke, no control. He managed to get Charlie's name out before a large, firm hand pressed down on his shoulder. George had eased himself out of his seat and now stood at Derek's back.

"Don't even think about saying another word son. Just collect your belongings and get out of here. I might be 70 years of age but if you so much as glance back as you go, I'll personally see to it that you get the hiding that has had your name on it for a long time." George's grip became stronger on Derek's shoulder and began to guide him to the front door. George let himself give Derek an extra hard shove as he forced him out through the door. Still The Local remained quiet. Not a word had been spoken in minutes. George shuffled back towards his chair, stopping only to reach over the counter to take Charlie's hand, "it's alright now love, we'll look after you here like we always have. Your life can start anew today if that's what you want." George knew Charlie wouldn't want a full discussion about what had just happened. Sharing a house with a wife and three daughters had taught him the value of knowing when to do nothing at all. "Give us a bar of the Galway Shawl there Larry and we'll start the sing-song early today. Even a wake can have a feckin' sing-song!"

Sitting down behind his pint once more, George looked over at Larry giving his party piece, and their traditional party starter, everything he had, with eyes closed too. He took a sip and as he replaced his glass he caught Charlie's eye. He didn't know how to convey the support of the customers and the support available to her, so he gave her a broad smile and a wink over at Larry. He wanted to see her smile and know that all his fellow customers would protect her like the daughter they saw her as.

Charlie gritted her teeth, wiped her eyes with her sleeve and forced a smile back at George. A new beginning had indeed been forged. She could feel the support of the Thursday regulars, who knew her so well and to see that not one of them was judging her for what had happened. But rather they were judging Derek. It went against everything she had imagined would happen over the past 14 years.

For the first time since 5th Year in school, Charlie could see the real benefit of growing up in a small community where everyone pretty much knew everyone else's business. She felt what it was like to have these people on her side and prepared to defend and protect her. If the community, of which this older generation was a good example, could see past her sin to the person inside then maybe she could convince herself that the church would welcome her back too. 'Fucking hell Charlie, one battle at a time is enough for you!' she thought to herself and then she carried on collecting empty glasses.

39.

"At long fucking last we've found a place that's open! They must all be Holy Joe's out here on a Sunday, not daring to open before half 12. For fuck's sake Barry stop pissing against the wall, I'm sure they'll have a jacks in here you can use. Even out here in Ballygobackward!" A quiet and peaceful start to Sunday morning in The Local was about to be well and truly taken away, replaced instead by the loud, crude and typical attitude and language of a group of lads out of Dublin. Paul and Padraig sat at the counter and made eye contact with each and every one of them as they hurried into the pub. The Local had always been a self-regulating pub and all the regulars and residents knew that. In fact they knew it so well that when a random group such as these lads barged in they were viewed as a novelty by the regulars as much as a nuisance.

"This'll be fun now son to see how Charlie deals with this" Paul whispered to Padraig conspiratorially.

"I know" Padraig whispered behind his raised glass. "She didn't look too hot herself this morning when I got in. She was probably at the same party as these lads last night!"

Charlie meanwhile was making a slow return to the counter with a glass of ice pressed to her temple. But when she caught Paul's eye as he straightened up and nodded in the direction of the door, she made sure to put down the glass and put on the game face.

"Morning lads, how are we doing today?" she asked as she scanned the group, sizing them up in no time at all; a couple of hyper rowdies, another couple asleep standing up, a potential vomiter and an aggressive one. Every single one of them pissed as newts though. Charlie's experience kicked in and overrode her hangover. The one who had been elected as the soberest outside and who'd been mouthing off as he opened the door stepped forward from the group. Charlie stopped him in his tracks before he could begin the order. Barry meanwhile had obviously finished his piss and joined his mates inside the pub.

"Look lads, it's simple you won't be getting any drink in here today. It looks like the party you were all at last night isn't long finished, am I right?" The hyper ones wanted to argue their case but Charlie could see that the sleepy ones seemed almost relieved. "Get yourselves on home lads, get a few hours kip under you and you'll be right as rain again but I'm not wasting my Sunday morning babysitting you."

"Ah but come on Mrs we'll be grand" Barry had decided to chime in but couldn't decide whether he was asking for something off a teacher, a barmaid or the little old lady whose garden his football was in.

"Listen it's not happening lads, I'm not minding you and I could probably teach you a thing or two about handling your drink but today's not the time. It was worth a try and I'd probably have done the same in your position but go on, head for the station."

Somewhat reluctantly they turned on their heels and left without much argument, except for the usual words and posturing. They had got the answer that most of them had expected and the sleepy ones seemed to get a little boost not only at the prospect of seeing their beds soon but at not having to lose face for it to happen. But just as the last soldier turned right to head towards the station, McCoy's was spotted across the road but away from the station. For some the prospect of a curer perked them up a bit, while other heads dropped as they realised showering, sleeping and a Sunday roast were being pushed from their grasp.

"They were so close to making it towards the station, now the two lads who were at the front are racing to be in front heading the opposite direction. God be with the days I had that sort of energy after a night on the sauce! Now all I get to do is come in here to serve you pair and the few stragglers in God's waiting room below. It doesn't seem fair really!"

"Ah what else could you ask for Charlie than to serve the two of us? We're a great laugh altogether! The morning will pass much quicker for you if we're here, especially with that hangover you're nursing today!"

"What hangover?"

"What hangover? Jaysus Charlie, who are you trying to kid? I'm drinking in here how many years now I've forgotten but you've never been able to hide your hangovers, I hate to be the one to break it to you Charlie. Back when you'd youth on your side you didn't get many hangovers but now it's so obvious I'd probably be able to guess exactly how much you drank last night and if it was more or less than last week?! Not to mention the big pint of ice resting against your temples and forehead for the 'migraines' isn't fooling anyone."

"You're one cheeky bastard Paul Forsyth! When I'd youth on my side? I'll still never catch up with you old man!"

241

"At least I know I don't have to take it personally now on a Sunday morning when you're lashing me out of it!" Padraig was enjoying himself for the first time in a long time and joined in with the banter.

"Hey, hey, hey, fuck off you!" Charlie responded, "You're only a blow-in and only here a wet day so don't be presuming you can take the piss like this fucker here alright?" Charlie threw her thumb in Paul's direction but all the while she was laughing with two men who less than a month ago she hadn't had a conversation with. "Just remember Padraig I'm the one who invited you up here to the top end of the bar and I can relegate you back down there just as fucking quickly!" Charlie tried to feign some sternness but she was also happy to be smiling properly for the first time in ages.

"It's good to see you smiling though Charlie" Paul added. "It's something we don't see often enough around here at all. Sure jaysus Padraig she's almost good-looking when she smiles isn't she?"

"Almost Paul, almost! Maybe if a squint a little it'll help?"

"Jaysus you're getting brave now son, taking on our Charlie. She'd eat you up for breakfast so she would."

"Fucking hell, I'm raging you two didn't bury the hatchet in each other the other week. You're going to be one hell of a double act annoying me aren't you?" Charlie watched the two men laugh together and then drink their pints at the same time. It had been a long couple of weeks for them all but she was glad to see the lads had each other to lean on for some support. 'If only I had someone to step up for me too' she thought, then we could all move forward.

"George was talking to me on Thursday in the jacks love. He was telling me about Thursday afternoon Charlie" Paul began, to the untrained ear it sounded like he was used to talking about feelings and emotions. "I can't believe what you had to go through all those years ago. But in fairness, George gave me the impression you were well able to handle that Derek by yourself when the time came?"

"What are you on about Paul? Did I miss out on the entertainment this week?" Padraig asked.

"Yeah you missed out on the sparks flying here on Thursday but in fairness I did too. You know the old lads that drink in here on a Thursday? Well they were settling in to update the phonebook when their hearts got a workout they haven't had in years. There should've been a queue of ambulances here for them all!" Paul turned back towards Charlie before he continued. "I never liked that dickhead Charlie, jaysus even back in the day I knew he was wrong 'un but I thought it was him just being a bit of a jack the lad, I never thought he'd do something so awful."

"Lots of people thought the same Paul but unfortunately I knew better all along. I just never knew how to deal with it and stand up to him."

"Who are we talking about here? And more importantly what did he do to you Charlie?" Padraig was struggling to keep and follow the thread of the conversation.

"Remember the gobshite that got between us a few weeks back son?" Paul asked

"The same fucker I told you to move away from in the bottom of the pub. I told you he was bad news and you shouldn't be hanging around with his sort. Well I'd first-hand experience of him and the horrible things he was and is capable of. When we were kids growing up in the town, he'd act the eejit and get into trouble here and there but I thought I'd found a kind side to him underneath all that. But one day not long before Christmas he showed me how cruel and vindictive he can be. He forced himself on me...."

"Fucking hell Charlie that's awful!" Padraig blurted

"That's not the end of it though because I was pregnant. It was such a horrible experience and I've spent 15 years or so trying to suppress the memory and find a way to move on. But believe it or not, this big lug beside you Padraig gave me the push I needed to follow through."

"Paul did? How the hell did he do that? I doubt being a grumpy old man has ever inspired anyone?" Padraig placed a hand on Paul's shoulder as he spoke; they were enjoying each other's company.

"No it's true Padraig, he did. He gave me the push to stand up to that prick and stop running from my past. I stood behind this very counter last Wednesday and watched a man put his family first and lay out the family history they knew nothing about. I saw a man who has barely shown an emotion of any kind in 15 years, bare his soul in front of his children. He showed me that there is nothing in our pasts we can't ever face up to and deal with.

So I decided to face up to my abuser, the single cause of all my shame, guilt and depression. I decided to stop running from what he did to me and put him out of my life. When he barged in to the Thursday afternoon OAP pints again, I was sure the time had come. It did help having an ex-Garda in George there too but I faced him down, I confessed to everyone what had happened to me and I've begun to try and move on. It's going to be fucking difficult but no more than the last 15 years. I'm not going to let my past control my present and my future. It's time I started living my life again. That's the way it's supposed to be."

Epilogue

"For jaysus sake Jack! Are you trying to impress her or knock her out? That's some aftershave you're wearing!"
"Bit rich coming from you Dad, don't you think? What was it in your day, Brut and Old Spice?"
Maura was sitting in front of her dressing table in the bedroom, listening to Paul and Jack trying to wind each other up. She recognised in Jack the same quick wit and charm, Paul once had, always ready with a smart reply or a put down. A mix of pride and happiness sustained the smile on her face.
The laughter, the slagging and the closeness had returned to their house. No longer were they living as individuals but as a family, a supportive and loving family. Barely six months previously Paul had been terrified of his children leaving home hating him. Yet now he and Jack were as close as good friends and though Louise had moved out to go to college in Cork at UCC, she came home on the train every Friday, looking forward to coming home and seeing her parents.
"Right, I'm out of here Dad I'll see you in the morning." Maura could hear every word but Jack still called up the stairs. "Mam? I'm heading out now; a cup of coffee around 11 in the morning would go down well ok?"
Maura wanted to reply but she burst out laughing at her son's cheek instead. Her laughter drifted down the stairs and sent Jack on his way in good spirits. Paul managed to get in one more warning as Jack slammed the door behind him. "Whatever about yourself make sure you look after your sister out there tonight, ok?"

"I won't!" Jack lied.

"Jaysus love, are you coming down at all tonight or are you staying up there?" Paul didn't move off his armchair to ask his wife, he merely roared up the stairs. Then he picked up the remote to un-mute the television.

Maura, meanwhile, took one last look in the mirror and smoothed her dress as she stood before she floated down the stairs and into the kitchen. "Did Louise have enough money for tonight? Will she be meeting up with Jack or are they out separately tonight?"

"I slipped Jack a few quid for both of them and I think they're going to meet up after the girls finish drinking in whichever house they're in." Paul responded almost as loud again, afraid that Maura wouldn't hear him when she reached the kitchen but by the time he was done, she was in the door jamb.

"No need to shout love, I'm right here!"

Paul finally took his eye off the television. "That you are Maura, jaysus you look beautiful, between the new colour in your hair and the dress, you look amazing."

"Well it's a rare enough thing to get a little dressed up and get out of the house for an evening!"

"Ah well I'm doing my best to change that. Come on we better hit the road or we'll be late. Coming up to Christmas, there mightn't be too many seats free!"

"You won't have to worry about that anyway Paul, they'll have your throne put aside!"

The Forsyth's were a little later than expected leaving the house, it was only a five minute walk to The Local but it was already gone half past before they left. There was a pre-Christmas chill in the air as they walked but Maura didn't need to worry. After pulling the gate closed, Paul reached out to take Maura's hand in his. They strolled hand-in-hand like a pair of love-struck teenagers. Late for their Saturday date night but completely happy and content with life.

Charlie spotted them as soon as they entered the pub, the door never opened without her somehow seeing exactly who it was. She smiled at the Forsyth's and started to pour Paul's pint. As he looked around the pub to see who was in, Paul spotted Padraig at the top of the pub waiting to be served.

"How are you getting on son? Did you have a good week? I hope you managed to hold on to a couple of seats for us."

"Howya Paul, yeah we got in a bit early so we got the table under the window as usual. I was so anxious to get up here so I left the house about an hour ago!"

"What are you like son? Jaysus I enjoy meeting you for a pint in here but if you're looking forward to spending Saturday night with me and Maura, I think you've got bigger problems!"

Padraig reached past Paul to plant a kiss on Maura's cheek. "You look really beautiful Maura, I'd ask if you wanted a glass of wine but Charlie has it poured and on the counter for you already. So I guess you'll be having it whether you want it or not. I held our usual table even on the Saturday before Christmas."

"You did your best son but there's someone sitting there now!"

"Just grab your drinks there Paul" Padraig began to explain, "grab them and follow me. Darling? These are my friends I was telling you about. Paul and Maura Forsyth, I'd like to introduce you to my wife Sinead."

CPSIA information can be obtained
at www.ICGtesting.com
Printed in the USA
LVOW04s1600260916

506251LV00024B/1079/P